THE HOLIDAY BRIDE

By
Ginny Baird

Published by
Winter Wedding Press

Copyright 2012
Ginny Baird
Trade Paperback
ISBN 978-0-9858225-7-6

All Rights Reserved
No portions of this work may be reproduced
without express permission of the author.
Characters in this book are fiction and figments of
the author's imagination.

Edited by Martha Trachtenberg
Cover by Dar Albert

About the Author

From the time that she could talk, romance author Ginny Baird was making up stories, much to the delight -- and consternation -- of her family and friends. By grade school, she'd turned that inclination into a talent, whereby her teacher allowed her to write and produce plays, rather than write boring book reports. Ginny continued writing throughout college, where she contributed articles to her literary campus weekly, then later pursued a career managing international projects with the US State Department.

Ginny's held an assortment of jobs, including school teacher, freelance fashion model, and greeting card writer, and has published more than ten works of fiction and optioned nine screenplays. She's additionally published short stories, nonfiction and poetry, and admits to being a true romantic at heart.

Ginny is the author of bestselling novels *The Sometime Bride* and *Real Romance*, and has just launched her "Girls on the Go" series, which premiered with *Santa Fe Fortune*. She's a member of Romance Writers of America (RWA), the RWA Published Authors Network (PAN), and the RWA Published Authors Special Interest Chapter (PASIC).

When she's not writing, Ginny enjoys cooking, biking and spending time with her family in Tidewater, Virginia. She loves hearing from her readers by email at GinnyBairdRomance@gmail.com and welcome visitors to her website at http://www.ginnybairdromance.com.

Chapter One

Lucy hoisted her waitressing tray high and snaked through the crowd at the packed diner. Paper Christmas decorations plastered the walls and plastic holly was draped from the counter to the floor. Customers hunkered forward over steaming cups of coffee and generous wedges of pie, as their heavy coats overburdened hooks by the door. Lucy spied a couple across the way snuggled giddily together on one side of a booth. Suddenly, the man involved slid from his seat and dropped to one knee. Lucy paused in her tracks, her heart thumping below the loud chatter. Though she couldn't hear his words, his intent was clear as he pulled a ring box from his pocket and took his companion's hand.

"Hey! Watch it, will ya?" Belle shouted, nearly crashing into her. Belle had worked here forever, and her years of experience were etched in her face.

Lucy lowered her tray, steadying it in her grip. "I'm sorry, Belle. I didn't see you coming."

Belle's eyes fell on the happy couple across the room, both now standing and engaged in a joyful embrace. "Maybe if you kept your eyes on *your* customers, instead of mine, you'd be more aware."

Lucy sighed, her gaze skimming the tiny solitaire on her left hand. It was hard not to think of Mitch and make a comparison. He hadn't even bothered to ask her officially. Instead, he'd just shrugged and said, *Well, you know what this means,* handing over the ring. "I'll try to be more careful."

4 *The Holiday Bride*

"You just do that," Belle said, raising her own tray and stepping past her.

Lucy swallowed hard, collecting herself. Though Belle came off as gruff, she wasn't all bad. Everyone here was cranky by now. They'd been working like crazy all season long. Here it was Christmas Eve, and business hadn't let up one bit.

Lucy adjusted the silly Santa hat that Gus had forced her to wear and pasted a smile on her face. She'd been on her feet for ten hours and every one of her muscles ached. One of these days, she was going to get a better job, one that allowed her to sit once in a while. From the looks of this crowd, she thought, trudging through the sea of elbows and clattering dishes getting tossed in bus buckets, that day wouldn't be anytime soon.

On the other side of town, William Kinkaid stood by the snowy window as his five-year-old daughter said her prayers. Springy chestnut curls spilled forth as she bent her head, fingers interlaced. "God bless Daddy and Justin, and Mommy in heaven..."

William felt the familiar ache in his chest, just as he did every time the kids mentioned Karen. It wasn't that he didn't want them to remember her. Maybe it was more that it was hard for him to remember her himself.

"Okay, pumpkin," he said fondly as she finished up. "It's into bed with you."

Carmella hopped into bed and scooted down under the covers. "Will Santa really bring me what I asked for?" she asked, looking at him trustfully with big dark eyes.

"What did you ask for, sweetheart?"

"Uh-uh," she said, shaking her little head. "It's a secret."

"Santa's not going to bring you *that,* fuzz brain," Justin called from the doorway. William turned to find his twelve-year-old son standing in the threshold.

"Be nice, Justin. And you go to bed, too. Or else, Santa won't bring you what you asked for either."

Justin shrugged and strode away, his shirttails hanging around the slouchy jeans that draped loosely on his lanky frame.

William returned his attention to Carmella, still waiting on his answer. "Of course, sweetheart. You bet. Santa will do everything in his power to bring you what you want."

Carmella grinned, settling her head on her pillow. Something crackled underneath.

"Carmella?" William asked, leaning forward to check and see where the sound had come from.

Carmella flipped over and hugged her pillow. "It's all right, Daddy. You don't need to see."

He studied her, stroking his chin. "Why don't I?"

"Because it will only make you sad."

William steadied his emotions, thinking his precocious little girl always had a way to read him. At times, it seemed she was five going on thirty-five. Maybe that was because she spent most of her time around much older folks.

"Your old man's pretty tough, you know." He extended a hand, expecting her to turn over her hidden stash. How bad could it be? A handful of pilfered candy canes? William resisted a chuckle, maintaining his stern daddy pose.

Reluctantly, Carmella pulled a stack of papers from under her pillow. William was stunned to see they were advertisements, torn from catalogues and magazines. "What's this, pumpkin?" he asked, fanning through them. There were pictures of families, and mothers with daughters, all dressed in the finest fare.

Carmella blinked, then said urgently. "I was looking at clothes, Daddy! Girls like fashion!"

William stroked his chin, and eyed her suspiciously. "So I've heard..." Something about this didn't add up. He didn't think pressure was that keen to keep up with labels in kindergarten. Although his mom had repeatedly warned him: *You can't have those children walking around like ruffians, William. For heaven's sakes, buy them some decent clothes.* That's where all the catalogues had come from. They were entirely his mom's idea. Though William didn't believe his kids looked *that* bad. He basically let them wear what they wanted, and always shopped at the upscale malls. "Well, if it's fashion you're after, we can hit the stores the moment they reopen after Christmas."

"All right," she said with a big, bright smile.

William kissed her on the head and said nighty-night, still feeling as if something were amiss. He'd really thought she'd wanted that enormous white teddy bear she'd already named Cubby. Hadn't she ogled it each time they'd passed the window of that store?

He switched off the light, as she snuggled contentedly under the covers. "I know I'm going to get it. I just *know*."

"And I'm sure you will, pumpkin," he said, smiling softly.

William turned and ambled toward the door with a heavy heart. He couldn't stand to disappoint his daughter. He hoped to goodness he'd gotten this Christmas right.

Lucy turned in a hurry, nearly crashing into Belle again. "Watch it!" the older woman shouted, clearly agitated. Even her patience was wearing thin, and Belle was long on patience. Lucy quickly backed up, but not in time to avoid splashing two new coffees down the front of her uniform. *This is great, just super,* she thought, on the verge of tears. Her last customer had stiffed her a tip, all on account of some burnt toast that she'd had nothing to do with. And now, *this.*

"Say, Luce!" the kindly older cook called from the griddle. "Why don't you call it a night? You've worked two hours over already!"

Belle offered to hold her tray as she dabbed her apron with a rag. "But this place is packed!" she told Gus, her voice cracking. Lucy hated that her tone betrayed her. She was only thirty-one and was supposed to be tough. At least as tough as old Belle here. She thanked the other waitress and took back her tray.

"Packed or no, it will go on without ya. Now, scat! Consider it an order." He motioned to Belle to take Lucy's tray back and Belle sighed with resignation.

"Sure, yeah. You go ahead," she said, accepting the mess. "Least you've got a life waiting on ya."

Lucy swallowed hard, wishing that were true.

"But first," Gus commanded, patting the counter, "come, sit. Woman can't live by stress alone."

Lucy gratefully took an empty stool near the register, feeling her tension ease. She hadn't even realized how hungry she was until Gus set the big stack of pancakes before her. "Fresh blueberry. Your favorite."

"What would I do without you?"

"Starve, more than likely."

He poured her a glass of milk as she lifted her fork and waited.

"Oh no you don't..." he joked, "you're not dragging me into that disgusting habit of yours."

"Please, Gus? It's Christmas."

He pulled a bottle of chocolate syrup from the fridge and set it on the counter with a thunk.

"There really *is* a Santa Claus," Lucy said, greedily uncapping the bottle and pouring. Before she could ask, Gus had produced a can of whipped cream and spritzed a sweeping circle onto her chocolate-covered flapjacks.

"Yeah, and if he's watching, the old guy is sick to his stomach."

"It's good," Lucy said, digging in. "You ought to try it." The blueberry confection coated in chocolaty whipped cream melted in her mouth like a warm bite of heaven. "Mmm. Delicious."

"Thanks, but I give Pepto-Bismol enough of a workout."

"You act like I'm the only person on the planet who eats this."

He studied her with a mixture of affection and amusement. "That, sweetheart, is because you are."

Her gaze trailed to the ancient tube television mounted in the corner. An old black-and-white rerun from one of her favorite nineteen-fifties shows was playing, the sort with the ideal intact family and happy mom and dad. "If only real life were like that."

"Yeah, but life ain't no TV show. Perfection like that only exists in—"

"I know, I know. Fairy tales."

"The Classics Channel is full of them. Maybe you should watch it less, and live a little more."

"God knows I'm trying."

"So, where's the lucky fellow tonight?"

"Working, as usual."

"Socking away the dough for that love nest of yours?"

"I guess," she said, knowing she sounded less than convincing.

"Somehow you don't sound so excited."

Her gaze panned back to the television. "Like you said, perfection only exists in fairy tales—and on the Classics Channel."

Gus cleared her empty plate. "Sometimes you've just got to take what life serves you up. Even if it gives you indigestion."

"Thanks, Gus," she said with a weary smile. She stood and grabbed her coat off a nearby rack.

"Any time, kid. You have a merry Christmas now."

"Yeah, you too."

The moment Lucy stepped onto the street, a frigid blast of air hit her smack in the face. She bundled her scarf around her head and neck and trudged down the street through the blinding snow. What had started as light drifts had turned into a heavy sludge that dropped from the sky in icy strips. At least she and Mitch had plans for tonight and she could look forward to a cozy evening indoors. While Mitch wasn't much on romance, he'd promised for weeks that tonight would be special. As soon as her shift ended, he'd be taking off from work as well, so just the two of them could spend the time together they so badly deserved.

Lucy was glad to see the lights from Mitch's real estate office burning brightly up ahead. He was always the last one working, though he maintained it was for a cause.

Lucy pressed through the heavy glass door, enveloped in a swirl of snow and sending its door chime tinkling. Whistling winds howled as she pushed the door shut.

Mitch didn't even look up.

Lucy strode to where he sat and set her gloved hands on his desk, palms down on either side of his laptop. "Um-hum," she said, leaning forward and hoping to get his attention.

Mitch looked up with a start, and removed the pen clenched in his teeth. "Sweet Merry Christmas, Luce," he said, studying the flakes stuck to her honey-blond hair. "You look like a blasted snow bunny!"

"That's because I *am* a blasted snow bunny. Haven't you even looked outdoors? It's really coming down out there."

Mitch craned his neck to peer over Lucy's shoulder. "So it is," he said with apparent surprise. "Sure wasn't doing that this morning."

"You didn't even break for lunch?"

Mitch angled toward her, trapping her hands in his. "Babe," he said, with serious brown eyes. "This is the big one." His cell rang and he motioned for her to wait.

"Magic Maker Mitch, at your service!" he said into the mouthpiece before flashing Lucy a grin. She knew his spiel so well by now, she could practically spout it herself. "Closing on the thirty-first?" he continued. "No problem."

Lucy's heart skipped a beat. "But Mitch, that's our—"

He quickly covered the mouthpiece to assure her, "I'll have this all wrapped up by six, no problem."

Lucy pursed her lips, wishing she could be sure. With Mitch she never knew. New Year's Eve wasn't some casual date. It was their—

"Can do, that's my motto! Four o'clock on the thirty-first it is!"

He ended the call and ran a hand through the stubby brown hair he always wore in a Marine's cut, though he'd never actually been in the service. *Makes the clientele totally trust me,* he liked to say, *real apple-pie-like.*

"Mitch," Lucy said, speaking past the lump in her throat. "December thirty-first is our wedding."

"Of course, I know that." He stood and pulled her into his arms, soggy coat and all. "That's precisely why I'm doing this. For you!"

"Me?"

"Baby," he said, tilting up her chin and meeting her eyes. "You've got to trust me when I say this is the big tamale. We're talking swimming pools, movie stars, the whole nine yards. Once this deal's cut, we'll get twice the house for our money."

"But I already told you, I don't need a big house."

He jostled her in his arms. "You just say that because you've never allowed yourself to believe you deserve it. But I know better, you hear? And I intend to see that you, little lady, get all the happiness you deserve."

Lucy's cheeks warmed with a hopeful flush. "You mean you've changed your mind about having kids?"

Mitch studied her with alarm. "Kids? Hoo boy, Luce. I was talking about you and me! I don't recall that discussion being on the table."

"That's because you keep taking it off," she told him. "It's important. A big thing we need to talk through."

"You bet, and we will," he said, releasing her. "Tomorrow, at my place. Turkey with all the trimmings!" He smiled sheepishly and lifted a stack of papers from his desk. "But first, I've got some files to go through."

"But I thought you promised tonight—?"

"I know, baby, and I'm sorry. Really I am. But this deal will be worth it. Just you wait and see."

"Yeah, sure," Lucy said, resigned. Every new deal was the big tamale... or taco... or enchilada, and Lucy was growing weary of Mexican food. She shoved her hands in her pockets, feeling let down. It was their last Christmas Eve as single people and she'd really hoped that they'd spend it together. "Won't I be seeing you later?" she asked with a tentative glance.

"Of course. You bet. I'm still planning on stopping over. Just as soon as I wrap up things here, and deliver those packages."

Lucy followed his gaze to a stack of neatly wrapped gifts by the copier. "What are those?"

"Just some things I said I'd take care of for a client."

Lucy checked the clock on the wall, thinking that he'd never make it to her apartment at this pace. Maybe if she helped out, she'd speed things up a bit, so they could at least enjoy one glass of eggnog in tandem before midnight. "What's the address? I'll take them."

"You'll what?" he asked with surprise.

"I said I'd take them, Mitch. Just let me know where they're going and I'll drop them off."

"Gosh, Luce! Are you serious?"

She nodded, then spoke under her breath. "Got nothing else to do."

"You're the best!" He took her by the shoulders and planted a big kiss on her lips. Then he scribbled an address on a post-it note and stuck it to the top package. "It's not too far from here. Actually, it's kind of on your way."

Lucy had barely gone fifty feet when she started regretting her decision. It was as cold as Siberia out here, and the sidewalk was slippery besides. She adjusted the bulky sack holding the packages in her arms, wondering what sort of client couldn't do their own Christmas shopping and delivery. Mitch really went overboard sometimes, forever banking on his zealous devotion paying off. If only he were a little less devoted to his work and a tad more attached to her, she would be happy. But what was happiness, anyway? Like Gus had just said, life wasn't some fairy tale.

Lucy blinked at the glare of headlights meeting her head-on. She was approaching a crossing, and the driver apparently didn't see her coming. He barreled straight ahead, obviously not spotting the stop sign, either. Lucy had been scurrying along, trying to make haste in completing her task, so she could get home. Now, she had to call herself up short and stop on a dime to avoid walking into the path of the oncoming car. She gripped the sack with a start as her sneakers skidded against slick pavement beneath her. Their soles were coated in a film of ice, lending her no traction at all. "Ohh, whoa!" she shouted, hydroplaning toward the intersection. She was sliding faster now, with no way to stop herself. Then, *bump,* she went over the curb and felt herself falling backward toward the sidewalk.

Taillights streaked away as the back of her head came down hard.

The last thing Lucy saw was a tiny post-it note fluttering high into falling flakes and twirling away, as sleigh bells chimed.

Chapter Two

William cinched the tie on his robe and paused at the bend in the stairs. Carmella raced down the steps ahead of him, dashing to the large beige sofa facing the fireplace. Two stockings brimming with goodies hung from the mantel.

"Oh boy, oh boy!" she cried, springing on her heels in a happy dance. Justin appeared on the landing beside his dad.

"What is it, fuzz brain?" he asked with a yawn.

Carmella looked up at them, her cheeks aglow. William had never seen her so excited. "He did it! Santa really did it!"

William descended the stairs feeling pleased with himself. He did know a thing or two about fathering, after all. "Well? Is it what you wanted?"

"Boy, is it ever," Carmella said with a happy gasp.

William strode around the sofa, feeling smug. Then, suddenly, he halted, nearly tumbling over the coffee table.

"Wow," Justin said, gazing straight ahead of him.

William stared in shock at the lovely blonde on the sofa who was clutching Carmella's teddy bear! She didn't look much over thirty, and was very reasonably put together.

The woman opened her eyes with a start and tried to sit, before quickly lying back down. "Where am I?" she asked with a pitiful moan.

"Don't you know?" Carmella asked, taking her hand. "Santa brought you home!"

She pushed herself upright, grasping the back of the sofa. "Home?"

"You're our new mommy!"

William stared at the woman, who stared back in shock.

"Our new...? Oh no, no, no, no, *no.*" William suspiciously studied his son. "Justin William Kinkaid, did you have something to do with this?"

"No, Dad! I swear!"

"I bet it was Eddie," William said, stroking his chin. "Eddie, from the bank. I gave that scoundrel our key to water the houseplants at Thanksgiving, and he never gave it back."

Blue eyes flashed beneath long dark lashes, as the woman took all of them in. "Do I... know you people?"

William strode toward the sofa and spoke in a coarse whisper. "Listen, missy, I don't know who you are, or what—"

"I don't either," she said, sounding alarmed. "How did I get here? Was I abducted?"

"Ab—*what?*"

"Why are you two whispering?" Carmella piped up. "I want to hear what she's saying."

"Ditto that," Justin added. "Ought to be a doozy."

William scowled at the woman, thinking this little practical joke had gone too far. "Would you mind having a word with me in the kitchen?"

She gripped the bear and scooted back on the sofa. "I don't know. Maybe I *would* mind. You seem a little unstable to me."

"Don't be afraid," Carmella said kindly. "Santa wouldn't send you to a bad place."

"Santa? But there's no—" the woman began before William cut her off with a silencing look. "...way he could have told me what a pretty little girl you are," she finished, picking up on the cue not to let the *there's no Santa* cat out of the bag.

"If you don't mind?" William said, motioning toward the kitchen door.

Lucy stood in the kitchen, her head still woozy. Her legs felt like spaghetti that had been way overcooked. She held on to the center island to steady herself as the man ranted on. He was impossibly irritated with her, and she hadn't a clue why. In fact, she was having a hard time remembering much of anything.

"Okay, we're away from the kids now," he continued, "you can drop the act." For someone so obviously agitated, he was terribly handsome. With that solid six-foot frame and those chiseled features offset by morning stubble, he almost looked like a star meant for television. But then, why was he wearing a robe? "I don't know what you mean."

"Listen, I don't know what Eddie paid you—"

"Isn't Eddie the one who hired the stripper for your birthday?" the boy asked from the threshold. He held a big bag full of packages and looked to be twelve or thirteen. From the smirk on his lips, he liked to think he was older.

The man's naturally ruddy complexion took on a deeper flush. "A *dancer,* son. She was a dancer. I thought I explained all that. Just what have you got in your hands?"

The tween cast Lucy an appreciative eye. "Looks like your mystery date brought gifts. Loads of them." He checked a tag and grinned. "By the way, her name is Bridget."

Lucy and the man exchanged glances, but all she drew was a blank. Bridget didn't sound quite right. Then again, it wasn't completely unfamiliar.

"Fine, fine," the man told the boy, "thanks for the update. Now could you please..." He motioned for his son to leave and the tween skedaddled. He turned his gaze back on Lucy and she noticed his honey brown eyes were dabbled with flecks of gold right around the irises. "All right, Bridget. Let's get one thing straight. There will be no disrobing in this house. Do I make myself clear?"

She set her hand on her hip, affronted. She might not recall much at the moment, but she was certain she wasn't a stripper! "Give a break," she said. "Do I look like a stripper to you?"

He scrutinized her, apparently deciding.

"Look," she said, "there's obviously been a big misunderstanding. I don't know someone called Eddie, and I certainly don't know any of you."

"Well then, there's no other explanation. You broke in here."

"Come on! I don't know a lot, but I know that I'm no thief. Listen, I'm just as upset about this as you are. Maybe more. I wake up on some stranger's sofa, whose kids think Santa brought me—"

"And we both know that's not true," he said, tilting his decidedly masculine chin.

"Oh!" Suddenly, all the commotion hit her and she felt incredibly light-headed.

"What is it? What's wrong?" he asked, his face softening with concern. Maybe, just maybe, he believed her and trusted she wasn't putting this whole thing on.

"My head. It's..." She reached for the back of her head and instantly winced at the pain.

He gingerly lifted his hand toward her scalp. "May I?"

She nodded, increasingly dizzy.

"No wonder you feel faint," he said. "You've got quite a bump back there."

Lucy stumbled forward and he caught her in his sturdy arms. "Bridget?" he said, searching her eyes. *He really is incredibly gorgeous,* she thought in the split second before the lights went out. And then, Lucy felt herself falling into someplace totally dark and warm.

William stared down at the woman who'd collapsed against him, at a total loss. What on earth could he do? He clearly couldn't leave her slumped over like this. As carefully as he could, he slipped one arm beneath the back of her legs and lifted her into his arms. Cradled against his chest, she looked almost like a princess from a fairy tale. Her hair was blond and fine, tucked back at the top with some pins, and falling in some sort of uneven arrangement around her chin. Her complexion was fair, although she looked even paler now that she'd fainted away completely. Ordinarily, he'd take her to the hospital, but he wasn't sure of his odds of getting into town with the snowstorm upon them and the one-lane bridge closed. He'd call the doctor first, that's what he'd do. And then start phoning around. The police, the missing persons bureau... She had to be on the level, and was clearly injured besides.

A moment later, William carted Bridget through the living room as Carmella sprang from her chair. "Where are you taking her?"

"Probably back to the loony bin where she belongs," Justin said from nearby.

"Justin!" William corrected sternly.

Carmella raced to the front door and flung herself against it, arms outstretched. "Oh no you don't!" she told her puzzled father. "Bridget was *my* Christmas gift, remember? No exchanges, no returns!"

"I'm not taking Bridget anywhere," he kindly told his daughter. "Except for up to bed."

Justin lifted an eyebrow, but William just cleared his throat and headed for the stairs. "You know what I mean, son."

"She's good, I'll give her that," Justin said.

"She's not playacting," Carmella retorted soundly. "She's just tired. Bet it was exhausting riding all the way around the world in that sleigh."

"Yes, well," William said, taking his leave. "I think I'll just take her upstairs and let her get some rest."

William carried Bridget to the master bedroom and tenderly set her down on the bed. As cautiously as he could, he removed one sneaker and then the next. Her instep dropped into his hand and he halted, looking up at her legs with a flush. She wore nylons and a short white dress marked with dark stains that appeared to be some kind of uniform. William hadn't thought about women's legs in a long time, and certainly hadn't been this close to any. Definitely none this lovely. He quickly lifted a throw blanket to cover them, and the rest of Bridget's womanly figure as well.

He caught a glimpse of Karen's picture on the nightstand and felt his face redden, suddenly overtaken with guilt. He hadn't looked at another woman since Karen died, and had honestly had no desire to. What with being a single dad and managing the bank, he scarcely had time for a female friend. He was nearly forty besides, and well out of practice with the ladies. With Karen, things had been easy. They'd been companionable college friends who'd become lovers, then later had married. He'd felt lucky to have been spared the trials and tribulations of playing the field that so many of his buddies purported to delight in, but secretly disdained. It really was a jungle out there, and William Kinkaid's swinging days were done.

Something sparkled on Bridget's left hand, and he realized with an odd sense of sadness that she wore an engagement ring. Well, of course she would, wouldn't she? Pretty young woman like that was bound to be taken. Was sure to have a wonderful life—and fiancé— waiting for her somewhere out there. And wherever they were, William was going to help find them. It was the least he could do for a stranger, especially at Christmastime.

"She's so beautiful," Carmella's soft voice rang out behind him. William turned in surprise to see his daughter had entered the room.

"Bet she escaped from prison," Justin said, trailing behind her.

Carmella puffed out her cheeks. "Did not!"

William shooed them out of the way and quietly shut the door. "Now, come on, you two. I'm sure she didn't escape from prison."

"Yeah. The elves made her," Carmella informed them.

"Elves don't make people, fuzz brain."

William shot Justin a look, and then stooped low to speak to Carmella. "Is that what you asked for, Carmella? A new mommy?"

"Oh, yes. And isn't she perfect? A little younger than I asked for, but I guess that's okay."

A lump welled in William's throat. "Sweetheart," he said softly. "I know how much you miss your mother. We all do." He pursed his lips a beat. "But I think that you should know—"

"There's no such thing as Santa!" Justin proclaimed with mirth.

The child gasped, pain streaking her eyes. "Daddy, say he's wrong!"

William huffed and glanced at Justin, agitated. "Downstairs. *Now.*"

Justin skulked away, saggy pants drooping, as Carmella clutched her teddy. "But he brought me Cubby! And a mommy! You said he was real. You wouldn't lie, would you, Daddy?"

William set his jaw, feeling like a big fat fake. He couldn't tell Carmella that Santa wasn't real and break her little heart. She still had so much of childhood left, and her childhood had been hard on her already. Growing up without a mother had left her longing for things he couldn't provide. William saw that now and felt awful about it.

"Of course there's a Santa," he said, drawing his daughter and her bear into a hug. "You bet there is." He pulled back and thumbed her nose with a smile. "You got your Cubby, didn't you?"

Chapter Three

One hour later, William lowered his voice and spouted into the mouthpiece, "What do you mean I have to wait forty-eight hours to report a missing person. I just told you, she's already here!"

He set down the phone and massaged his temples just as the doorbell rang. Cheery voices and laughter rang out from the foyer as Carmella raced into room.

"Grammy and Poppy are here!"

William sighed, wondering how he was going to explain Bridget to his parents. They were overbearing enough when he led the life of the unencumbered single dad. Who knew how they'd take the news of a stranger landing on his sofa?

He walked toward the front door and helped his mother with her coat. She was neatly prim as always, in a crisply ironed skirt and buttoned-up blouse. His father was a mess, as usual, with none of his patterned items matching. "Mom! Dad!" William said, greeting them both with hugs. "How was the trip? Any trouble getting here?"

"Well, the walk was a little slippery," his mom said.

"Other than that, it went just fine," his dad finished for her.

William supposed it helped that they lived next door. Otherwise, with the storm pelting, they might not have made it.

Emma leaned forward and whispered in his ear. "Carmella says Santa left something on your sofa..."

"Something life-size," Grant chortled with a grin.

"Actually, it's not like that at—"

"Sure it is, Daddy!" Carmella butted in. "You said so upstairs. Just after you took her to bed, remember?"

Emma fanned her face with her purse as William reddened. "I don't really think this is appropriate," she hissed under her breath. "Not with the children—"

"He's a grown man, Emma," Grant cut in. He leaned in toward William. "But your mother's right, son. You should have asked her to leave before the kids got up."

"No, he should have asked her to *wait* until after the wedding," Emma said a little too loudly.

William croaked, *"Wedding?"*

"Oh boy!" Carmella crowed. "She'll look just like my Bride Barbie! Wait until you see her!" she said, shooting her grandparents a sunny smile.

Justin guffawed and William cupped his mouth with a hand. His parents were nearly to the stairs, his mom led by Carmella.

"Mom! Dad! Before you go up there—"

"She *is* decent, son?" his dad asked.

"She's just like Goldilocks," Carmella said.

Grant studied his son with admiration. "A blonde, eh? Well, why not."

Carmella tugged at her grandma. "Come on, but shhh... She's sleeping."

"Mom, wait!" But it was too late. They were already to the landing. William sighed and chased after them.

Justin gallantly rushed ahead, holding open the door for his grandparents.

"Very nice, Justin," William said under his breath. "Ultra helpful."

"Oh my yes," Emma said. "Lovely, really lovely."

"Of course, you can't see much with that blanket in the way," Grant quipped.

Emma turned to William. "Does she always sleep this late?"

"Not a drinker, is she?" Grant wanted to know.

"Please," William said in hushed tones. "Let's all go back downstairs. Mom and Dad, I've got some cocoa for you in the kitchen."

Justin triumphantly shut the bedroom door. "Sounds good. I'll come, too."

"Adult cocoa, Justin. Not for you."

Carmella looked hopeful.

"Or for you either, pumpkin."

"Can we open some of our presents?" Justin asked slyly.

"You bet," William said. "Just don't touch any of the ones brought by you-know-who."

Emma snatched the bourbon bottle from her husband and poured another liberal dose into her cocoa mug. "Oh, dear. This won't do at all."

Grant drained his mug, then set it aside. "Aren't you a little old to be picking up strays?"

"Look," William said, "I don't know what else to do! The police say no one has filed a missing persons report. I tried the hospital, too. But nobody's called there looking for her, either."

"Maybe you should take her to the hospital," Emma said seriously. "Maybe she's not *right*."

"The fact that she can't remember anything doesn't make her a psycho, Mother. Besides, you saw what it's like out there. Nobody's going anywhere until the plows get through."

"What about Dr. Mass?" Grant asked.

"I phoned him, too." William checked some notes on the table. "He gave me some instructions about waking her up every hour. Checking her pupils with a flashlight."

"So you're just going to let her stay here?" Emma asked.

"Dr. Mass says that–unless she takes a turn for the worse–he'll see us in his office in the morning, assuming the streets get cleared."

His mom tapped the side of her mug with neatly trimmed fingernails. "I still don't know if this is such a good idea. A damsel in distress... a lonely widower..."

"It's almost two o'clock on Christmas Day," William said. "I can't just toss her out in the snow!"

"No, I probably wouldn't toss her out of my bed, either," Grant said thoughtfully.

Emma swatted his arm.

Grant leaned forward with a conspiratorial whisper. "Say, what if she's escaped from prison? That would give her plenty of reason to forget who she is!"

William huffed with exasperation. *"She is not on the lam, okay?"*

Both of his parents pushed back in their chairs and stared at each other.

"Don't you think the cops would have mentioned it?" William asked, a slight edge to his voice.

William couldn't believe it. His dad almost looked disappointed. "Yeah, I guess you're right."

"Besides," William added, "she doesn't exactly look like the hardened criminal type."

Emma shook her head. "What about the children? How are they taking it?"

William frowned. "Carmella thinks Santa brought her."

Grant chuckled and William cast him a cursory glance.

"And Justin?" Emma asked.

In the next room, Justin eagerly pawed through Bridget's gifts. "I say we open all of them."

"You heard what Daddy said."

"Yeah... don't touch! So, I won't. I'll just open and peek inside." He yanked off the gift tag, hooting. *"For Koochie, for us to be naughty and nice..."*

"Koochie?" Carmella puzzled. "Do you think that's for Daddy?"

"One way to find out!"

He tore back the wrapping of a long box and Carmella lunged forward. "Justin!"

Before she could stop him, he'd dispensed with the rest of the paper and flipped open the lid. "Well, well, well..." Justin fell back whooping holding up a skimpy black-and-red lace teddy.

Just then, the adults entered the room.

"Why son," Grant said discreetly to William. "You buy that getup for Goldie?"

"Goldie? Hey, no! Wait!

Carmela stuck out her bottom lip. "No, Poppy. These are *from* Bridget." She purposefully collected the lingerie and deposited it with William. "Here, Daddy. I think this is for you."

William held the lace teddy, which dangled down in front of him. "No, honey, I don't think it's my size." If someone had stuck hot coals to his face, it couldn't have felt any warmer. Then he looked up to spy Bridget on the stairs, and felt himself combust from heat all over.

Lucy stopped walking and gaped at William holding a racy teddy and standing beside the Christmas tree. His face was the color of cinnamon, while Carmella pouted and the tween rollicked with laughter on the floor.

"Hello, dear!" a neatly dressed older woman called.

A man with abysmal fashion sense stood beside her and grinned. "You must be Bridget!"

"You're awake," William said, his voice cracking.

Frankly, this moment seemed a fine time to turn around. "No, actually I'm—"

"Sleepwalking?" Justin asked.

Carmella shook her head at her brother. "She's not sleepwalking, you Dumbo. Can't you see?"

"Why don't you come on down here and join us?" the older man said.

"Yes, dear," his wife agreed. "We'd like the chance to get to know you better."

That would be ideal, if only she had a way to understand herself. Who was this family, and how had she gotten mixed up with all of them? She recalled the sofa, remembered waking up here this morning quite well. It was all that came before that was a blur.

William shoved the lace teddy in his pocket with an embarrassed look. "Do come downstairs, if you're able. Do you need help?"

"No," she said uncertainly. "Thanks. I think I've got it."

A little while later, they sat around the family dining table where William carved a large turkey. Lucy had learned his parents were named Emma and Grant, and that the tween's name was Justin. Justin was slightly snarky, but Lucy supposed that came with the territory. Little Carmella, on the other hand, was simply adorable. She was so intent on Lucy being her *Mommy,* Lucy hadn't known what to think, or say, about any of it. While she'd gathered from the conversation that William had lost his wife some time ago, she wasn't sure how long it had been or under what circumstances. How hard that must be on William, handling this all on his own.

"White meat or dark?" he asked, meeting Lucy's eyes. But she truthfully didn't know. Lucy shrugged and Emma laughed, warmly patting her hand. A light mix of 1940s jazz played in the background. The music was comforting, and familiar, to Lucy at once, and yet—she couldn't place it.

"Don't worry, dear. It will all come back, eventually."

"The trip to the doctor's sure to help," Grant said.

"Doctor?" Lucy wondered.

William laid another slice of turkey on a platter. "I forgot to mention. I'm taking you to see Dr. Mass tomorrow."

Emma smiled reassuringly. "He's been our family physician for years."

Lucy felt her face warm. They were all being so kind to her. Had to be the Christmas spirit. "You don't know what it means to me, how nice you've been. I mean, I could have wound up anywhere, really. There are bound to be terrible places out there."

"Yes, right," Grant said.

"Bound to be," Emma added.

Dinner passed with Emma and Grant asking the grandkids what they'd been up to, and how their friends were in school. Everyone seemed to get on reasonably well, even William with his parents, despite their eccentricities. Serving plates circled round and round until Lucy was sure she'd eaten enough to hibernate for winter.

"More stuffing, dear?" Emma asked, hovering a brimming ladle over her dinner plate.

"Oh no, I couldn't," Lucy said. "I'm stuffed!"

"Tell us about the elves," Carmella said sweetly.

Justin grinned in her direction. "Yes, do tell us about those elves. Are they ordering from Victoria's Secret now?"

William and Grant turned on him at once, parroting together, "What would you know about Victoria's Secret?"

Carmella looked around the table. "Who's Victoria and what's her secret?"

Emma gave Grant a hard elbow and spoke in low tones. "What would *you* know about Victoria's Secret?"

Grant coughed loudly, as William cleared his throat.

"I'm sure Bridget has better things to talk about. Don't you, Bridget?"

He met her gaze, and Lucy's heart stilled. With him sitting there, and her sitting here, at opposite ends of the table, she could almost imagine them as husband and wife. And what a marvelous husband he'd make, too. He was accomplished, and settled, she thought, glancing around at the comfortable place. Not rich, but well off enough, and boy did he ever seem to love his family. From the happy feel in the room, the emotion was mutual. Not only that, he was easy on the eyes.

Way too easy. Lucy tucked the hand wearing the engagement ring in her lap, wondering if the guy she planned to marry was half as grand. A sultry rendition of Billy Holiday singing "All of Me" played in the background. *Take my lips, I want to lose them... take my arms, I'll never use them... How can I go on without you...?*

William stared at her expectantly, and Lucy realized he was waiting for her to say something.

"This stuffing *is* delicious," she said, suddenly lifting the serving bowl. "I think I *will* have some more."

"Do you cook much, dear?" Emma asked.

Lucy realized she was making a glutton of herself, nervously heaping mound upon mound on her plate. She stopped and looked up. "Um... cook?" Now, that was something she was used to being around. But, doing? Hmm. "Honestly, I can't exactly tell you. But I do know this, I'm totally used to being around food."

William grinned at her, oddly charmed by this. "Anything in particular, or everything in general?"

Lucy thought hard, willing even the tiniest tidbit to come to mind. Her eyes fell on a candy dish of green-and-red-wrapped holiday chocolates sitting on the sideboard. "Chocolate," she said brightly, knowing that was right. "Anything—and everything—chocolate."

Carmella appeared inordinately pleased. "No fooling? Daddy loves chocolate, too."

Justin lowered his eyebrows. "Yeah. He does the most disgusting thing with—"

"Justin, knock it off," William said, plainly embarrassed.

"Yes well, enough of that," Emma said. "Just let me clear the plates and I'll serve dessert."

"Bodacious bourbon pecan?" William asked.

Emma nodded.

"Make mine a double!" Justin said.

Lucy felt awkward not offering to help. "Here, let me take some of these," she said standing. At once, her knees buckled, sending her back into her chair.

"I think you'd best stay off your feet a bit longer," William said with a kind look. "At least until your legs feel steady."

Lucy met his eyes and her cheeks caught fire. He was so kind and caring. With that sensible banker haircut, she might never have known it just passing him on the street. But in here, all cozied up with his family, she saw William for who he really was. He was the sort of man who looked after people. It was a feeling that Lucy hadn't known in a long while. That much, she believed was true. Even if she couldn't trust in anything else.

By the time coffee and dessert were over, Lucy had gathered her reserves and was feeling much better. She'd insisted William let her dry the dishes, and after a bit of lighthearted banter, he'd given in.

"You don't stay put very well, do you?" he asked, as she finished up.

"Please, William. I want to... need to do something to help." She set a clean pot on the counter and capped it with its lid. "The dinner was delicious, thank you."

He studied her with earnest brown eyes. "And I want to thank you, too. Thank you for playing along with Carmella. It would break her heart if she knew the truth."

"I'd sure like to know it. I'm hoping the doctor can help tomorrow."

He leaned back against the counter, studying her. "You know, I don't believe in that Santa bit, of course, but I'd sure like to know how you got in my house."

"Yeah, me too. You say everything was locked up tight?"

"As a drum."

"Maybe there's a rusty basement lock, or unsecured window?"

"What kind of father do you think I am? I double-check this place every night. It's just like Fort Knox."

Lucy drew a breath. "Well, I certainly didn't drop down the chimney."

He met her eyes and his gaze lingered. "At least we've agreed on that."

The seconds ticked by as Lucy watched him watch her, her heart pounding. She didn't know this man from Adam, but still, when she was with him, she had an uncanny sensation of being home.

"Still nothing doing on the memory?" he asked.

"Except for some weird little details, like knowing I love chocolate, I just draw a blank." She hung her head. "I feel really terrible. I've ruined everyone's Christmas."

William reached over and gently raised her chin in his hand. "Don't you go worrying about that. You haven't ruined our Christmas at all. But someone out there is sure to be having a rotten night." He glanced down at her engagement ring, then once more met her eyes. "Someone's bound to be looking for you."

A few miles away, Mitch checked the wall clock in his real estate office, cursing out loud. It was snowing even harder than yesterday. He hadn't even made it home last night, despite his four-wheel drive. He'd had to sleep at the office. Mitch stared through the plate-glass window at the pounding snow, knowing his chances of getting out of here now were slim to none. But heck, he had lots to take care of anyway. He could get a jump on those closing papers, and snooze in the break room when he needed to. Yeah, there was a plan, he thought, taking another swing of eggnog from the quart carton on his desk.

He scooped up his cell and dialed Lucy's number.
Hi, it's me. Leave a message at the beep.

"Hey, sweetheart. Merry Christmas. It's me, Mitch. Say, I really hate to do this to you again. But Luce, if only you knew the size of this deal. I'm serious. This one is the grand tostado. I mean, *loaded.* We'll have everything we always wanted, just you wait and see. The two-car garage, a whole closet full of clothes just your size. Luce, you'll even be able to cut back on your hours at the diner. Maybe quit your job completely.

"The only thing is, hon, I've got to get this contract faxed by midnight. Now, I know this is a holiday and all, and I feel so totally terrible about you spending it alone. But, I swear, I'll make the whole thing up to you. Next year will be completely different."

Out on the porch, William said good night to his parents. He'd tossed on his coat so he could speak to them in confidence, but the down parka was a poor barrier against the biting wind. "Mom, Dad," he said, as Grant wrapped himself in his big, brown scarf, "I want to thank you both for everything. The gifts were really terrific."

"Yeah, especially the pretty blond one," Grant said.

Emma tugged at her gloves, adjusting their fit. "What are you going to do with her?"

"Like I said, I'm planning on taking her to the doctor tomorrow. Maybe he can help us figure out why she can't remember."

"Or *what* she can't remember," Emma said. "I want you to be careful, William. Now, I know she seems nice... But sometimes the quiet ones turn out to be the most dangerous."

"Your mother's right, son," Grant said. "You really don't know anything about this girl. Are you sure you want her spending the night? This isn't college, you know."

"I appreciate your concern, both of yours. Really I do. But I can take care of myself."

His mother met his eyes. "It's the children we're worried about. Little Carmella really has her hopes up. We had no idea."

"I know, Mom," William said sincerely. "I had no clue, either."

A fire blazed in the hearth as Carmella snuggled up against Lucy, who read to her on the sofa. *"And laying his finger aside of his nose and giving a nod, up the chimney he rose..."* Carmella's eyes drooped and she cooed happily, gently fading into slumber as Lucy uttered the final lines, *"Happy Christmas to all, and to all a good night."* Lucy quietly closed the book, yawning herself. It had been such an eventful day, and who knew what tomorrow would bring? At the moment, she was cozy and warm, and way overstuffed with stuffing.

Justin looked up from a wing chair beside the Christmas tree, where he'd been engrossed in a handheld game. "You act like you actually know something about it," he said bitterly.

Lucy glanced down at the book, then met his eyes. "Well, I do. I mean, this story, of course. It was always one of my favorites to read." She wasn't sure how she knew that, but she did. *What is it about this place? This room?* "Right here, by this fire."

"Yeah, right."

"Justin," she asked, her eyelids growing heavy. "Just what is it that you don't like about me?"

"The same thing I don't like about all girls. You're weird. In fact, you're the weirdest. If you think I buy that *Santa dropped me down the chimney* business..."

She wanted to stay awake, really she did. She needed to talk to William about tomorrow, and sleeping arrangements for tonight. But the firelight was so soothing. She and Carmella together felt so right. It took her back to an earlier time, a time when the world was safe and family meant home. Even Justin's snarking couldn't combat the lull of the Sandman, beckoning her to drift away. A song came back, a lullaby, she thought... her mother's voice, rich and warm. And then, she felt her body sag into the sofa, all tension letting go.

When William reentered the house, he encountered an idyllic scene. Bridget and Carmella dozed together on the sofa, *The Night Before Christmas,* by Clement C. Moore, clutched in Bridget's hand. It was an old edition, one his parents had read to him as a child many years before.

He quietly hung his coat on the rack, not wishing to disturb them. William swallowed hard, resisting the warmth in his eyes. He couldn't recall having seen Carmella so contented in a long, long time. At least that made one of them, William thought, noting Justin's glum appearance in the wing chair nearby. He played his new video game with intensity, yet his expression was sullen.

"Time for bed, Justin," William said softly.

"But, Dad..." he protested

"Up!" William commanded, thinking it had been a full day for all of them.

Justin rose begrudgingly, casting a wary eye on Bridget. "Who is she really?"

"I don't know, son. But I'm sure as heck going to try to find out."

"Yeah, well, you'd better. Before she does any more damage around here."

"Damage?"

"Just look at them, Dad. How do you think Carmella's going to get over this? She's already lost one mom."

"Yes, son. And so have you."

"Here's the different between me and the fuzz brain. I don't want another mom any time soon. The one we had before was good enough to last me."

He stormily trudged upstairs, leaving William confounded. Justin was at such a hard age, William didn't know how to handle him half the time. And lately, he'd been more and more out of sorts. Having Bridget intrude on his holiday apparently hadn't sat well with him, either. But William needed to work on the boy. It was good for him to understand that charity came first, at the holidays especially. It wasn't like Bridget had chosen to come here. She was just as confused about her circumstances as the rest of them were.

Well, best to get everyone settled for the night so they could move on with solving things tomorrow.

William leaned forward to scoop the sleeping Carmella into his arms, then suddenly he pulled back. He studied the portrait before him, a deep melancholy taking hold. They truly were a picture together, Carmella in her springy curls and Bridget with her arm wrapped protectively around the little girl. William stood there for a long while, firelight lapping at his face. He crossed his arms over his chest, trying to stem the tide of his emotions. But they welled within him, anyway. And, in that moment, William understood that Carmella hadn't been the only one hoping for someone else in this house. In his heart, he'd wanted someone, too.

Chapter Four

Lucy was called out of deep slumber by a piercing white light. She sat up with a start to find William hovering above her with a flashlight. "What are you doing?" she asked, pulling the covers to her chest.

"Checking your pupils." He grimaced apologetically. "Doctor's orders."

Of course, she remembered now. That part, anyway. "Sorry," she said, settling back on the pillow and opening her eyes wide. "I forgot."

He angled the beam toward her, causing her to squint.

"Still nothing doing on the memory?" he asked.

She blinked as he turned off the flashlight. "Not a thing. I mean, other than everything that's happened here."

"Hmm."

She watched him study her as fine light filtered in through the window. "Is that the moon out there?"

"Lucky for you, we've had a break in the storm," he said with a smile. "I'm sure I'll be able to get the SUV out tomorrow."

"Oh," she said, wondering why that notion depressed her. Of course she wanted to go the doctor and learn what was wrong with her. This wasn't her house; it was theirs. And they likely wanted her out of it as soon as possible. She brought her hand to her cheek, mildly pained at the thought. Why did the idea of feeling unwanted ring so familiar?

"Bridget," he said, as her solitaire glinted in the moonlight. "There *is* a man in your life, isn't there? Somebody waiting for you?"

"I'd like to think so, yes," she said, unable to resist the ache in her heart.

His gaze lingered on hers and for a moment she suspected his heart ached, too.

"That's what I figured," he said.

"William?"

"Yes?"

"What's that disgusting thing you do with chocolate?"

He bellowed a laugh. "Your memory's not all bad, now is it? I'll never tell." He stood from where he'd sat on the edge of the bed. "Now, lie back down and get some rest. I'll be back to check on you in an hour."

"Is that a promise?"

"Yes," he said in a way that made her believe it. His eyes trailed to a photo of a pretty brunette on the nightstand. He picked up the frame a bit awkwardly, and took it with him. "I'll just... move this downstairs," he said.

Lucy snuggled under the covers, thinking what a happy woman she must have been to have someone like William for a husband. "William?" she said, as he slowly shut the door.

He paused and looked at her, picture frame in hand. "Thanks."

William sat on the living room sofa with a guilty heart. He'd brought a pillow and a blanket downstairs and had taken care to wear a robe, as he knew he'd be checking on Bridget later. He lifted Karen's photo from the coffee table and addressed it as if she were there.

"You don't know how much I miss you. How badly all of us do..."

His gaze slowly panned toward the stairs. Here he was with another woman in the bed that he and Karen had shared. Although it wasn't like he was up there *with* her. William swallowed hard, trying not to imagine what that might be like, he and Bridget together. She was so soft and womanly, with that curvaceous body and those sensuous lips. And her eyes were as blue as the heavens. They were an angel's eyes, really.

William fretfully stared down at the photo in his hands. "Forgive me, honey. I didn't mean it. There could never be anybody for me but you. I could never go there. Not in a million years... Not unless the gods sent me an earth-shattering sign." He settled down on the sofa, laying the frame facedown on the floor beside him. "Like that's going to happen."

William awoke the next morning to the smell of bacon frying and coffee brewing. He quickly sat up and swung his feet to the floor, trying to place where he was. The living room, that's right. That's where he'd slept, or gotten some semblance of sleep anyhow. Not that he regretted going up to check on Bridget. In fact, he'd sort of looked forward to it. Didn't matter that he'd had to set his cell to wake him hour after hour. The truth was, even when he'd been sleeping, she'd occupied his dreams. Once or twice, he'd awakened with a start because he'd thought he'd felt his arms around her. In reality, it had just been a throw pillow. William felt himself flush at having these thoughts, especially in light of his late-night promise to Karen.

He stood and something crunched under his slippered feet. William looked down in horror to see he'd smashed the glass on Karen's picture frame. He sat back down and lifted the broken frame in his hands. Karen's smiling face gazed back at him. *"An earth-shattering sign?"* he mused. No way. No earthly way. Clearly it was coincidental, him breaking the glass.

Noises sounded from the kitchen. Someone was cooking in there. William carefully picked the errant shards off of the carpet and set them on the broken frame, which he laid on the coffee table. Then, he slipped on his robe and headed to the kitchen to investigate.

Lucy whisked about the open space, attempting to put together a very fine breakfast. She had bacon on the stove and bread in the toaster. Next, to find the eggs. She whirled toward the refrigerator, nearly colliding with William as he entered the room.

"Good morning!" he said with surprise. His gaze traveled to her bare legs and quickly back up to her eyes. He'd left her one of his shirts to sleep in, but plainly had forgotten about it until he saw her wearing it skimming her thighs, its cuffs rolled up. Lucy had washed out her short dress and it was hanging to dry in the bathroom. That, along with her undies. She'd planned to dash back upstairs and get dressed before the family had awakened. A rash of heat enveloped her as she feared for a second that William might know she'd gone Commando. But no, that was silly! He couldn't possibly guess. He didn't have X-ray vision.

"Hello," she said smiling tightly. His eyes really were flecked with gold, she could see that quite clearly now, and my, were they gorgeous. A man built like that was particularly dangerous in a robe, not to mention that sexy morning stubble. Lucy's knees buckled slightly, and he reached out a hand to steady her.

"Bridget?"

What was it about that name that still felt wrong. "Huh?" she said, noting his waist tie had come loose and his robe gaped slightly. Beneath it he wore plaid pajama pants and no shirt, just a broad and muscled chest sporting a perfect smattering of light brown hair.

"Are you sure you should be up doing all this?" he asked, glancing around.

"Oh yes, I really am!" she said, turning toward the coffeepot, needing to redirect. "I'm feeling so much better. Honestly." *What* had she been doing ogling William's pecs? Is that the sort of woman she was? One that took advantage of every opportunity to pounce on a man? She had pounced before, hadn't she? She lifted a mug to pour, spotting the ring on her hand. Of course she had, rightly so. "Coffee?" she asked weakly.

"Coffee would be super, thanks." He glanced down and saw that his robe had slipped. "Sorry," he said a bit uncomfortably, before retying it and covering that marvelous chest.

She handed him the mug and he took a sip. "Delicious, thank you."

"As long as I was the first one up, I thought I'd make breakfast."

"I still don't know if it's a good idea for you to be so active."

"Why don't we let the doctor be the one to decide about that?"

"All right." He studied her thoughtfully over the rim of his mug. "This is really nice. I haven't had anyone make coffee for me since... in a very long time."

Fine lines creased his brow, and Lucy suspected he was remembering his late wife. "I'm really sorry about your wife, William. Has it been long?"

He pursed his lips a beat, then met her eyes. "Karen died of ovarian cancer three years ago. It came on very quickly. There was nothing the doctors could do."

The pain in his eyes was unmistakable. He clearly wasn't over it. But then, how could he be? What an awful thing that must be, to lose someone... Lucy felt a sharp tightness in her chest, stirring some recognition. "You loved her very much, didn't you?" she asked softly.

"More than she knew."

Lucy hated to think of someone as wonderful as William being alone. Certainly there were boatloads of women who would eagerly snap him up. "You'll find somebody else. One day. Don't you think? I mean, some day when you're ready."

"To tell you the truth, I've never really thought about it."

"Well, Carmella apparently has. And I'm betting Justin has, too."

"Justin?"

"Boys his age need a woman to talk to just as much as a father."

He set down his mug and leaned into the counter. "How do you know so much about kids and family?"

"Probably from watching too much late-night television," she said, laughing.

"The Classics Channel?" he asked with pleased surprise.

"Why, yes! That's right! I know it is!" She stared at him and grinned. "You mean, you watch those shows, too?"

"Well, sure." He cleared his throat. "I mean, when the kids are with me and they insist."

Lucy struggled with a murky memory, the odd refrain coming back to her. "But real life isn't like fairy tales."

William blinked, then asked with mock offense, "Who told you that?"

This part, Lucy knew absolutely. "Gus!"

"Gus? Who's Gus?"

"I don't know. Someone from my past. Yes, that name. It's important, for certain."

William drew nearer. "Your father? Brother? Fiancé...?"

Lucy felt mildly sick to her stomach. "Fiancé? No!"

"Well then?"

"Argh! This is driving me nuts! It's like something's right around the corner, but I can't quite grasp it. None of this makes sense. How can I remember the Classics Channel and not even recall my own name?"

"It's Bridget, isn't it?"

"Is it?"

"I have no idea, sweetheart. But I can tell you one thing. Whatever that old cynic Gus had to say was way off base."

She watched him wide-eyed, still stuck on the fact that he'd called her sweetheart. *Sweetheart.* Ooh, she liked the sound of that, especially coming from his warm, expressive mouth. Was she swooning? Was that even a word?

"Because let me tell you something, " he continued, stepping closer, "when a guy finally meets the right girl, the whole world becomes a fairy tale."

Their eyes locked and Lucy's heart skipped a beat. Yep. She could buy that, every word of it, and she was staring straight at a prince.

"Bridget?" he asked, his gaze diving into her. He smelled so good and manly, like sandalwood and spice. Oh God, she didn't remember this. Couldn't recall ever feeling this way. Surely, she would recall emotions like this.

"Huh?"

"Do you smell something burning?"

A smoke alarm blared and Lucy brought her hands to her head and yelped. Black smoke curled from the toaster, which immediately burst into flames. "Oh no!" A split second later, the frying pan caught fire.

William looked around in shock. "Jesus." He raced beside the refrigerator and yanked a fire extinguisher from its holder on the wall. In a flash, he'd pulled its pin and doused the toaster and the whole stove in white foam.

An hour later, Lucy sat in a family-style breakfast place with William, Carmella, and Justin. The snow had let up long enough for the plows to get through, and the one-lane bridge leading to the Kinkaids' suburban neighborhood had been cleared. The day's forecast called for nothing more than light flurries.

"I still don't understand why we couldn't have breakfast at home," Justin complained.

Carmella looked up from the kiddie placemat she'd been coloring with crayons. "Because the elves didn't build in cooking skills, silly."

Lucy turned toward the little girl. "Build in?"

"Sure, you know, like how some dolls have built-in talking machines. Things like that."

Justin eyed Lucy suspiciously over his glass of orange juice. "Yeah, and others are made plain lucky."

William shot Justin a stern look. "I'll ask you to remember your manners."

A waitress appeared with a notepad and Lucy felt a twinge of familiarity. "Do I know you?" she asked, puzzling at the woman.

The gal, who looked to be in her fifties, turned her eyes on Lucy. "Don't think so, love." She returned her attention to the table. "You folks ready to order?"

"Bridget?" William prodded.

"I'm not really sure what I'd like. Why don't you all go first?"

Justin set aside his menu. "I'll have the Western Omelet with extra sausage and hash browns."

"I'd like the chocolate chip kids stack," Carmella said. "With bacon."

William twisted his lips, scrutinizing the menu. "Could you make mine the tall stack of blueberry pancakes?" He glanced sheepishly at the waitress. "And bring some chocolate syrup, please?"

Lucy abruptly set down her water, sloshing it sideways. "Make that two of those!" Her eyes met William's. "With whipped cream."

His jaw dropped, before his lips tugged into a grin. "Can't forget the whipped cream," he told the astounded waitress.

"Are you folks serious?" she asked with a disgusted look.

Lucy and William locked eyes.

"Yes," she said.

"Most definitely," William followed.

"Suit yourselves," their waitress said, "just don't expect me to bring the Tums."

She departed as William stared at Lucy, dumbfounded. "I can't believe you like your pancakes that way."

"But only on blueberry," she said, feeling herself smile.

"Only on blueberry," he said. "There's something about that fruit and chocolate mix."

"Yes!"

"How did it happen for you?" he asked.

"I'm not sure." She studied the table a beat. "It may have had something to do with my mixing up the pancake syrup and—"

"The chocolate meant for your milk?"

Her eyes flashed in recognition. "I think that's right."

"No way," he said, sipping from his coffee. "That's what happened to me, too."

Carmella turned smugly to Justin. "You see, Bridget's made just the way she's supposed to be. Just right for Daddy."

"Find me a bucket. I think I'm going to hurl."

Lucy tried not to be stung by Justin's constant barbs, searching her heart for understanding. The boy was hurting more than he let on and covered those wounds in a patina of sarcasm. It must be terribly hard to lose a parent at such a young age. In some ways the absence of his mom troubled him even more than Carmella, because he'd had more time to spend with her before she'd gone. Lucy felt a lump in her throat as an old familiar ache arose. She couldn't quite place it, but it was there deep inside, telling her not to judge Justin too harshly. His father, however, filled another role.

William sighed and frowned at his son. "I'd appreciate it if you revised your attitude. Especially since I need your help later this morning."

"Help?"

"I want you to watch Carmella—"

"But, Dad—"

"So I can take Bridget to the doctor."

"Why's Bridget going to the doctor?" Carmella's face clouded over. "Is she sick?"

"Who knows?" Justin said with a smirk. "Maybe she's pregnant."

"Pregnant?" both William and Lucy said together in shock. He stared at her.

"No, no, I don't think so," she said, laying a hand on her belly.

William shook a scolding finger at Justin. "You, young man, have been spending *way too much* time online."

A little while later, William sat with Bridget in the physician's office. She'd already had a complete checkup in private. Now they were awaiting the results of the examination. "Dr. Mass? Please tell me," Bridget asked with concern, "is it bad news?"

The big-bellied, white-haired physician removed the stethoscope from around his neck. William noted it still had the same small stuffed reindeer attached that it had sported for years. "Please, call me Chris, dear," he told Bridget with a warm smile. "All my patients do. Except for ones like him" he said, tilting his head toward William, "who I've been treating since they were in diapers."

"Well, don't keep us in suspense," William urged.

Dr. Mass steadied his small circular glasses above his plump round nose. "I'm afraid it's a clear-cut case of amnesia. The bump on the back of her head, combined with the memory loss, can point to nothing else."

Bridget lifted her brow with concern. "How long will it last?"

Dr. Mass stroked his snowy beard. "That all depends. Sometimes these things resolve themselves in a matter of days. Then again, they can drag on for months."

"Months?" William blurted involuntarily. He'd been prepared to help Bridget out temporarily. But for the long term? He just didn't know. He met her blue-eyed gaze and thought he heard angels sing. William shook his head, thinking he'd had one too many hit of bourbon pecan pie. But wait a minute... That was *yesterday*.

"Have you tried the police?" Dr. Mass asked him. "The missing persons bureau?"

"Everything I could think of," William assured him. "I plan to follow up more when we get home today."

"That's good, son," Dr. Mass said. "Might even want to try one of those Internet postings. I hear they can be very helpful. Someone's bound to be looking for her."

William glanced at Bridget, regret brimming inside him. "I'm sure of it," he said, wondering where that sentiment had come from. It's not like she could stick around forever. She had a life—and a fiancé—to return to, after all.

"Chris," Bridget said. "It's very strange. There are some things I remember, little things really, that don't make any sense. But the bigger picture is all a blur."

He eyed her with understanding. "Par for the course, dear. The memories should all come back, but won't necessarily surface in the expected order.

"The good news is that you're perfectly healthy, other than the amnesia. The scans were clear and all your tests came back negative. The best I can suggest for the short term is that you engage in things that might spur your memory."

"Such as?" William asked.

Dr. Mass turned toward Bridget. "When you arrived at the Kinkaid house, did you have anything with you? Anything at all?"

Chapter Five

Lucy perched on the edge of the bed in the master bedroom. William shut the door and came and sat beside her, a stack of presents in hand.

"You're right about doing this away from the kids," he said.

Lucy had insisted on utmost privacy for the rest of the gifts' unveiling. Judging by the item in the package that Justin had opened, she couldn't imagine what might be in these other boxes. Hopefully, nothing too scandalous for her *Koochie*. Boy, that just seemed wrong. Who on earth calls somebody that?

"Ready?" William asked, passing her box number one. She felt her face warm and he reddened in return.

"Maybe I should... um... Open them alone?"

"I was a married man once, you know."

"Sure," she said, smiling tightly and feeling as if her cheeks might burst from the pressure.

"This one looks interesting," he said, peering at the tag. "*My love will set you free.* I wonder what that means?"

Lucy shrugged and peeled back the wrapping with trepidation. It was as if, with each layer of red and green foil, she was stripping away herself. Oh my God, she thought, staring into the box. Perhaps she was a stripper, after all!

William chuckled and raised a pair of fur-lined handcuffs from the unfolded tissue paper. "Well, well." He studied her in a new way that told her maybe he was reconsidering her profession, too. "Any flashbacks?" he asked with a wry twist to his lips.

"Not a one!" she declared a little too loudly. All at once it felt terribly hot in here. Was that because she was used to going without clothes? Lucy cringed, thinking that forgetting might have its merits.

He handed her another box. "Try again?" he said, both looking and sounding mildly amused.

She peeked at the tag and then stood abruptly. "Oh no, I don't..." There was no way on earth! "I think I'd better open this one in the bathroom!" She grabbed the box and scurried out of William's sight, barricading herself behind the door. Seconds later she flung open the package and wailed, *"What kind of woman am I?"*

William sat up with a start on the bed. Perhaps there was more to Bridget than he'd imagined. She certainly seemed to have a secret side. Not that he minded, or that it was really any of his business. He was only interested in helping learn who she was, sparking her memory, that's all.

Bridget burst back through the bathroom door, hastily gathering the rest of the packages in her arms.

"What are you doing?"

"Hiding these away somewhere where the children won't find them!"

"That bad?" he asked, wide-eyed.

"Oh, much worse," she assured him, without surrendering any details. "Do you have something like duct tape?"

William appeared taken aback. "Duct tape? Is that something else you like to—?"

She turned bright red. "Oh God, no. It's nothing like that! I just want to close these securely. We can't take any chances."

He handed her the fur-lined handcuffs, which she flung back in the box like they carried something communicable. "Hmm, yes. I see what you mean."

She stared at him, mortified. "Wait a minute. You don't actually believe those are *mine*?"

"No," he said, ribbing. "I know they're for Koochie."

She heaved a sigh, big blue eyes brimming with tears. "This is so very awful. I don't see how this has helped one bit."

"Listen," he said standing and taking the packages from her. "There could be dozens of reasons why you had those presents with you."

"Really?" she asked, looking hopeful.

"Why, sure," he said, unable to think of any.

"So you're not judging me?"

"Judging? Sweetheart, I don't know you well enough to judge you."

"But if you did, would you?"

She tilted up her chin and William realized in a flash that she was within kissing distance. It wasn't like he'd done it in a long time, but he clearly recalled the instinct. He guessed it was like riding a bicycle, only softer... more curvy... and feminine. Heat warmed the back of his neck. "Would I?" he asked, lost in the moment.

"Judge me," she repeated, dark eyelashes fanning wide.

William drew a breath and counted to ten, telling himself not to lose his head. Here he was with a beautiful woman beside a large comfy bed on a wintery afternoon. *And my children are right downstairs,* he reminded himself, swallowing hard. *With my mother and father!* "No, absolutely not. Never." He took a giant step back, drawing the gifts in toward his chest. "I mean, never in a bad way. Listen, Bridget, I'm a very fair-minded individual. Whatever other people choose to do in their personal lives is their business, not mine. I mean, as long as everyone's a grown-up and agrees."

"Yes, that's what I think too," she said, taking a step back of her own.

"I think you're right, and we'd better find a place to stash these."

"Good," she said with a nod.

Downstairs on the living room sofa, Carmella snuggled between her grandparents as her Grammy read her a storybook. Her Poppy sat on her other side, reading the sports section of the newspaper.

Emma turned the page and Carmella looked up with a pout. "Why did they go upstairs?"

"They needed some privacy, dear," Emma said.

"For what?"

Grant chuckled. "Likely discussing North Pole secrets."

"But I want to hear how Santa got her down the chimney!"

Grant glanced at Emma. "I'd be interested in hearing that myself."

"Shush," she told him.

Carmella stared at Emma with big, brown eyes. "Bridget's not sick, is she Grammy?"

"Oh no, dear."

"Dr. Mass says she's healthy as a horse," Grant said. Then he added under his breath, "Not even pregnant."

Emma glared at him, but Carmella just said, "Darn!"

Her grandparents exchanged glances, then looked at her.

"I was hoping for twins," the child explained.

William entered Justin's room to find him working at his computer. Justin glanced in his dad's direction, then closed a series of pop-up boxes.

"Justin, I'm going to need your help with something."

"Sure thing, Dad," Justin said, still furiously clicking the mouse. "Name it."

William scrutinized his son a beat, and then met the boy's gaze. "Do you know how to build a Web page?"

"Piece of cake."

"Good, because I was thinking we could put up one of those Internet postings."

"An advertisement?"

"Well, no. Yes. Something like that. What's the name of that local site where you can get anything and everything?"

"Dave's List?"

William nodded soundly. "That's the one. Do you think they've got a section for Lost and Found?"

Justin smiled securely. "No worries, Dad. You can leave *everything* to me."

William sighed with relief. "That's my boy. Now," he asked, "What do you need?"

"We probably need a picture. We can use your digital camera."

"Great thought. I'll go and get it," he said, turning away. "Bridget, too."

"Uh, Dad?" Justin called after him. "I was just thinking... Maybe it would help if Bridget modeled some of that stuff she brought with her? You know, make her more recognizable?"

William shot him a stern look and shook his head. "Don't think so, Justin."

A big-busted woman strode into Mitch's real estate office with a combative air. She slapped her purse on his desk and Mitch looked up at the bleached blonde in a leopard print coat smacking her gum. She removed her dark glasses to glare at him. "What's the big idea?"

"Bridget!" he said with surprise. "Ain't you a sight for sore eyes. So, you decide on that six mil mansion?"

"No, you slimy cheat. What's your excuse this time? Still haven't gotten over the fact that I dumped you for Roger?"

He blinked at her. "I don't know what you're talking about."

"My packages!" she cried with dismay. "You promised you'd bring them by."

"I did! I mean, I sent... Wait a minute. Are you saying you never got them?"

She pulled herself upright on her petite frame and studied her manicured nails. "I knew you didn't have it in you to be a gentleman, despite all that stuff you said." She lifted cat-green eyes to his. "You're still getting back at me, ain't ya?"

"No, Bridget! I swear! I'd never—"

She licked her lips and he squirmed in his chair. "Though you're still pretty good to look at, Mitch-o. Despite your conniving."

She leaned forward, her coat gaping to reveal the low-cut blouse beneath it.

Mitch gulped. "And you're still looking good, too. How's Roger?" he asked with a squeak.

"Getting bored with marriage, I think." She inserted herself between Mitch and his desk, then purred in a sexy whisper, "I always thought you worked too hard."

"Ditto, sweetheart," he said with a hard stare.

She flinched. "Ooh, was that a cut?"

Mitch rolled his chair back a foot and spoke matter-of-factly. "Listen, Bridget, I've got stuff to do. I'll find out about those packages ASAP. Okay?"

"Yeah, well, you'd better. I spent over three hundred smackers at The Naughty Shop!"

His cell rang and he reached around her to snag it off the desk. "Magic Maker Mitch at your service!"

Bridget rolled her eyes and sauntered toward the door. "Magic Maker, hoo. You'd think that new gal of yours could find someone better."

Chapter Six

As William bent down to lift his morning paper off the stoop, he heard a mounting commotion. His raised his eyes in disbelief to the pandemonium around him. Their quiet residential street was flooded with vehicles and hordes of men were pouring into his yard. There were jocks dressed in sports uniforms, Wall Street types in suits, military men, construction workers, guys in tuxedos carting flowers. Holy cow! William's jaw dropped as he stared up at the noisy helicopter hovering above and some lunatic parachuted in for a landing. A knight on a white horse galloped in through the front gate, trailed by a rowdy group, a few of them on motorcycles. The mass stormed toward the house, calling out to him in competing voices, "She's mine! She's mine!"

William raced inside, sweat beading his brow. He quickly bolted the door, seconds before its chime sounded. *Ding-dong... ding-dong... ding-dong!* The landline rang next, trilling loudly on the hall table. William lunged for it, picking it up. "Bridget? No, she's still sleep—What? *What?*" He held out the receiver in shock, then pressed it back to his ear. "Well, I don't know whether she'll give an interview."

A pounding sounded outside the door. "Mr. Kinkaid! This is WKVX News! Can we get a statement?"

William hung up the phone and strode toward the stairs, taking them two at a time. An instant later, he burst into Justin's room, popping the boy on the head with his up newspaper. "Justin William Kinkaid," he said. "I want to see that Web page you built, and I mean *now*."

William gaped at the computer screen. It was Bridget all right, only better. She was very scantily dressed in some sort of sexy elf outfit, jingle bells dangling from strategic places. William frowned and stared down his son as the boy flushed red.

"*Sexy Cyber Mom Seeks Home?* Justin! Just what kind of junk have you been reading?"

"The personals?"

"But, son! You gave our home address! A MapFinders link, even!"

"You told me to list contact information."

"I meant an e-mail address, telephone number, maybe. Not this!" He shook his head and stared again at the computer screen. "We don't even *know* if she's got kids, for heaven sakes."

"She's the right age, isn't she?"

William blew a hard breath, his eyes glued on Bridget's photo. "How did you do that? You know she wasn't wearing that when I took the picture."

"Computer program. Really simple." Justin gulped. "Even allows enhancements."

"So I see." William ran a hand through his hair, wondering how he was going to get out of this mess.

"I thought the jingle bell tassels were a nice touch," Justin said with an impish grin.

Carmella pressed into Lucy's room with a worried frown. "What's all that noise?"

Lucy quickly released the curtain she'd pulled back to peer outside. "I'm not sure."

"Then what were you looking at?"

"Just some birds out on the lawn!" she said above the hum of copter blades lifting away.

"Birds? But all of those have flown south for the winter."

Carmella strode to the window with determination and threw back the curtain. "Oh my! Who are all those people?"

"I don't know," Lucy said, standing behind her. There was an incredible crowd out there, and it appeared testosterone heavy. In fact, the only woman Lucy saw seemed to be a television reporter. She held a huge microphone and spoke through a broad smile to a couple of cameramen by a truck.

Carmella spun toward Lucy, gripping her legs. "You don't think they heard about Santa, do you? And they're coming to take you away? Sort of like they do with aliens?"

Lucy bent low to hug her. "Oh no, sweetie. Don't you worry one bit. Nobody's taking me anywhere. I'm sure those fellows are all just here for a visit."

Carmella looked her in the eye. "It's awful early for visiting. We haven't even had breakfast yet."

Lucy studied the little girl, the truth paining her. Sooner or later, Carmella was going to have to know. From the looks of the horde outside, *sooner* was going to come first. "Carmella," she said, "About Santa... There's something I think you should know. I don't really believe—"

"Of course Santa brought you!" the child said, throwing her arms around Lucy's neck. "Even Daddy said so!"

Carmella hung her head, then looked up with misting eyes. "You know, when Mommy died, I was very little. Just two. So I barely remember her at all. But, I do remember one thing. She used to sing to me."

"I'm sure it sounded beautiful," Lucy said kindly.

Carmella gulped, wiping away her tears. "So when... you know... I asked Santa for a new mommy, I was kind of hoping that..." She stopped and met Lucy's gaze. "That you would..." Her voice trailed off, her little chin trembling.

Lucy sat on the bed and pulled Carmella into her lap. "Shh... Shh, now. Everything will be all right. I'm sure soon enough Santa will send just the right mommy for you."

"He already has." Carmella looked up with pleading eyes. "Sing to me? Please?"

"But I'm not sure I know any songs."

"They must be in there somewhere. The elves wouldn't have messed that part up."

At the senior Kinkaid house next door, Grant perused the paper while Emma poured him coffee. "What's all that commotion, dear?" she asked.

"I don't hear anything," he said. Then again, Emma suspected he was going deaf. She glanced at the television on the built-in desk in the kitchen. There was some sort of reality show on. *That's odd,* Emma thought, *generally at this time we see the morning news.*

Grant lowered his paper to take a sip of coffee. An instant later, he spat it back in his mug. "That's William's house!" he spouted, staring at the television.

"Well, so it is!" Emma said in shock.

On the old black-and-white tube set, a farmer on a tractor bulldozed through the crowd in the street. He wore a straw hat and a big chest plaque stating *Bridget or Bust!* "Let me through! That's mama's mine!" he bellowed, barreling past the reporter extending her microphone.

Emma drew a hand to her mouth. "Oh my!"

Grant set down his mug and stood. "We'd better get over there and see what's going on."

They pulled on their coats and rushed outdoors, where the situation looked even more overwhelming than it had appeared on the small screen.

"It's like the whole world's gone crazy," Emma said with a gasp.

"Crazy for a certain blonde, I'd say."

"Gracious," Emma cried, "Is that a real set of armor?"

They elbowed through the crowd, as Grant spoke in agitated tones. "This is worse than Mardi Gras in New Orleans!"

"How do you think these fellows got wind of Bridget?"

Grant shook his head and pressed ahead. "Don't know, Emma, but I'm hoping William does." He parted the crowd with his hands, shouting gruffly. "Let us through! We're the parents!" A hush fell as heads swung in their direction. Emma's heartbeat picked up a notch. "We've got to get out of here," she told Grant, as someone in a paratrooper outfit raced toward them.

"Please, sir!" he petitioned Grant. "Can I have your daughter's hand? Sir!"

"Not *her* parents," Grant grumbled, trudging ahead. *"His!"*

Emma scurried after him. "Best to try the back door," she said.

"Probably safer," Grant agreed.

William struggled to collect his thoughts on how to deal with this. He'd have to address the thronging masses somehow, and *who knew*? It was possible Bridget's betrothed was among them. William hoped he wasn't one of the loony ones. Several of the contenders seemed slightly off kilter. But perhaps that was just at first glance.

William peeked back out of Justin's window, deciding his first impression wasn't all bad. Hang on. Were those his parents cutting through the crowd? Good. It appeared they were headed for the back door. He'd need to go down and let them in. But first, he'd have to check on Carmella. He hadn't seen her or Bridget all morning. They couldn't have possibly slept through this?

"Wow," Justin said, eying the lawn. "Dave's List is pretty effective, huh?"

"You and I will square up later," William said sternly before leaving.

He passed Carmella's room, noting that her bed was empty. He strode toward the master bedroom, but slowed his steps at the sound of singing. Bridget's melodious voice rose in a sweet tune, *And if that mockingbird won't sing, papa's gonna buy you a diamond ring...* William halted and peered around the doorframe to spy Carmella cradled on Bridget's lap. The little girl sighed happily, her tiny frame molded against Bridget's. Neither one had seen him, so he quietly slipped away, fighting the fire in his eyes. They were a pair, the two of them. If only Carmella was right and there really *was* a Santa Claus, he could convince himself this portrait was more than make-believe.

The doorbell chimed once more downstairs and William realized he'd better get moving. He had to meet his parents around back and get them indoors before one of the new reporters who'd just arrived discovered them.

Emma blustered in the door, trailed by Grant. "What on earth is going on?" she asked, removing her hat and shaking it out.

Grant quickly turned to bolt and chain the door. "Yeah, what?" he asked, his cheeks ruddy from the cold. There'd been a brief lull in the snow, though apparently it was long enough to allow all the marauders through. The light sprinkling that had started back up was obviously doing nothing to dissuade them.

"It's Justin," William said, out of breath from racing down the stairs. "It seems that the Internet missing-person posting he designed revealed a bit more than we hoped for."

Justin, who'd been standing nearby, quietly slunk away.

Emma's sympathetic gaze followed him. "Oh now, I'm sure he didn't mean it."

"I'm sure that he did," Grant said removing his coat. "The boy's older than you think, Emma."

"Yes, well, I plan to talk to him more about that later." William glanced through the door window to see more suitors storming the house. "But for now," he said, quickly shutting the blinds, "what are we going to do?"

Grant parted two blind slats to peer between them. "We could make a run for it."

"Very funny."

"I'm serious!" Grant told his son. "Out the back way and around to our place."

"Don't kid yourself, Dad. The backyard's filling up, too."

"Have you called the police?" Emma asked.

"Yes," William answered, "but they said they already had a few officers on the scene. Didn't mention they were carrying corsages!"

Emma studied her son with kind brown eyes. "Do you think any of those men might actually know her?"

William sighed. "I'm afraid there's only one way to find out."

The trio looked toward the hall as Bridget and Carmella entered the kitchen.

"Who are all those people out there?" Carmella wanted to know.

William glanced at his parents. "Just some nice folks who've come to see Bridget."

"I knew it!" the child cried, wrapping herself around Bridget's legs. "It's just like *E.T.*" She looked up. "They're coming to take you away!"

Lucy's heart pounded at the implausibility of it all. Could Justin's Web notice really have sparked this pandemonium? She'd made a wreck of the Kinkaids' holiday ever since coming here. And now, things had actually gone from bad to worse.

"No honey," William said. "They only want to talk to her, that's all. Bridget won't be going anywhere..." He paused, shooting Lucy a telling look. "Until she wants to."

Carmella studied him with moistened eyes. "By why would she want to? She's *ours,* Daddy! You said so! Santa brought her to *us.*"

William heaved a breath and Lucy dropped to her knees to address Carmella at eye level. "Don't you worry, sweetheart. I have a feeling everything will work out just fine." Despite the ruckus outdoors, perhaps some good would come of it. Maybe her intended was one of the men who'd come to whisk her away. Somebody good and kind like William, she thought, warming under the heat of his stare.

William pulled his gaze from hers to address his daughter. "Why don't you stay in here with your Grammy and Poppy and have some breakfast?"

"If I have to," Carmella said, regretfully letting Lucy go.

"Mom? Dad?" William asked them. "If you don't mind? Pancake mix is in the cupboard."

"Of course," Emma said, helpfully heading for the stove.

Lucy walked to the living room window and peeled back the sheers. "There are even more of them than before! Bless Justin. He must have built quite a Web page."

"Oh, I wouldn't go blessing him just yet," William said flatly. "I think you should know the boy built a... very explicit ad, urging the man who knows you to come and take you home."

"Explicit how?"

William swallowed hard. "You were scantily clad in items that looked like they came from some of those boxes. He used some sort of photography program."

"Oh!" she cried, her cheeks coloring.

He leveled her an apologetic look. "Justin will be punished for it."

"Oh, no. I don't think you should... I mean, just look at the results!"

"Yes well," he agreed, following her gaze out the window. "One could certainly claim the ad was successful."

She dropped the curtain and turned to face him, an unexpected melancholy taking hold. "I suppose this means I'll soon be out of your way." If it was possible, he appeared even more handsome than he had the day before, small flecks of gold warming his light brown eyes. "You must be relieved."

"No," he said stepping forward. He paused and seemed to collect himself. "What I mean is, Carmella will really miss you."

Lucy's heart warmed at the mention of the little girl. She was so sweet and trusting, and had cared for Lucy immediately in that hopeful childlike way. Lucy would have to be made out of stone not to start feeling some emotion for the child as well.

"She's a very special little girl," she said.

"Yes." He studied her a prolonged beat. "Bridget, I have something to tell you. I heard you earlier, singing to Carmella upstairs."

Lucy felt her cheeks flame and dropped her chin. "Oh. I'm afraid my voice is—"

"I thought it sounded heavenly," he said.

Slowly, she raised her eyes to his. What was it about him that sent her heart all out of kilter? "Well, I don't know when... Can't exactly recall singing before."

"And still you felt at home?"

"Yes."

William stared down into Bridget's big blue eyes. If he weren't careful, he feared he'd tumble right inside them and get lost swimming there forever.

"Can I ask you something?" she asked.

"Anything," he said, his voice gone husky.

She tilted up her chin and he had that overwhelming sensation again that he needed to kiss her. Kiss her like he was damn sure he could do, and do right.

"Did you always know you wanted to have kids?"

"For as long as I remember," he answered.

"Yeah, me too," she said. "Just somehow I never thought I'd really have them."

"You? Why not? Dr. Mass says you're as healthy as they come. Apart from that little, you know." He playfully tapped his forehead and smiled.

"It's just something I can't remember," she said, shaking her head. "Silly, probably."

"Well, somebody's going to be awfully lucky to have you as a mother... someday. When the timing is right."

She looked at him and grinned. "And Justin and Carmella are very lucky to have you."

Something pounded on the front door as a man's voice shouted. "Say! Can we get this show on the road!"

"Yeah, and look how lucky I am to have Justin," William said with a wry twist to his lips.

"Do I really have to meet with *all* of them?" she asked, clearly overwhelmed. How he wished he could rescue her from this, but he didn't really see a way. If Bridget were his fiancé and missing, he'd be crazy with worry, no doubt. He didn't think he'd don a suit of armor, but that wouldn't dampen his urge to up and carry her away. William swallowed hard, realizing he was the one getting carried away. Totally swept up in some alternate reality where Bridget could actually be his. But she wasn't, and as the man in charge, it was his duty to look after her. Even if that meant helping her find the man she was destined to be with forever.

"I suppose you ought to look at them, at least. I mean, how else are you going to know?" he said.

She frowned and glanced at the door. "Oh William. It's just so much. There must be two hundred men out there!"

Maybe more, he thought, thinking he spied a small figure through the sheer curtain covering the window. That couldn't be Justin outdoors? Positioned at a table by the gate? "Well, we don't have to do it all in one day," he said, his attention back on Bridget, who was now standing in the threshold. "We can have some of them come back again tomorrow, if you'd like."

"Do you mean it?" she asked with a hopeful gaze.

"Why sure, or the day after that." *That's right, just keep talking, William. Why not go on and admit you'd prefer that none of them return until well into the New Year?*

She blushed sweetly, fine wisps of honey-colored hair framing her face. "But I've already taken up so much of your time. Been so much of an imposition."

He moved forward without thinking and took her by the elbows. "Oh no, you haven't."

His eyes locked on hers, then simultaneously they both looked up to see they were standing below the mistletoe. Bridget stared down at her hand, her diamond glinting in the early light. William released her and abruptly stepped back.

Bridget anxiously twisted her engagement ring. "You're right. I'll need to look at all of them."

"Yes. I suppose you should."

William tugged on his parka as he walked through the kitchen. "Has anybody seen Justin?"

Emma turned from the stove as Grant buried his face in the paper. "I think he went outside, dear."

"Out in *that*?" William asked peering through the back door window. Just as he'd predicted, the backyard was also flooded with interested suitors. But the figure he'd spotted and thought was his son was around front. "What on earth is he doing?"

"I'm not sure," Emma said, absentmindedly flipping a flapjack.

"He said he was selling lemonade!" Carmella proclaimed between mouthfuls.

"Lemonade?" William queried. "But it's December!"

From behind his splayed paper, Grant just shrugged.

William pressed his hand atop the sports page, lowering it to face his father. "Dad? Do you know something about this?"

Grant coughed lightly. "I don't see what's so wrong with a little ingenuity."

William twisted his lips in thought, deciding something didn't add up. And wherever the math had gone faulty, his dad was sure to be involved. He generally was. "I think you should come with me," he told his father.

"But it's snowing out there!"

"Don't be such a big baby," Emma scolded from the stove. "Pull on your parka!"

William cut his way through the crowd, Grant reluctantly trailing along. "Excuse us! Coming through!" William called as two reporters and several men sprang at him. *"I said, no comment,"* he told the persistent news angler.

When they got to the gate, William could scarcely believe his eyes. There sat Justin, all decked out in his leather jacket and shades, holding court at a folding table he must have dragged out of the garage. A poster stuck to the fence behind him boldly stated, "Pay to Play: 10 Bucks!" There was a coffee can at his elbow stuffed with cash, and William watched as a beleaguered groom inched up to the table and dug a hand in his pocket.

"Got change?" he asked, holding out a twenty.

Justin lowered his shades and solemnly shook his head.

"Didn't think so," the man grumbled shoving his bill in the can.

"Hey! Wait!" William called, snatching the cash out of the can and handing it back to him. "There's no charge here."

He turned his gaze on Justin, who slunk down in his chair and cast a panicked look at Grant over the rim of his glasses.

"You, young man," William said with a shake of his finger, "are in *deep*."

"Really, son," Grant added. "What were you thinking?"

"But Grandpa!" Justin gasped. "Charging an admission fee was your idea!"

William huffed and turned toward his father. "Both of you, in the house, please. Now."

Chapter Seven

A few hours later, Lucy yawned on the sofa. They'd been at it all day, only breaking briefly for lunch, which Emma was kind enough to make. One by one, William had escorted each man in the house and asked for his credentials. After he'd supplied reasonable identification, the guy was asked to remove his hat, helmet—or whatever—and take a seat. All of the Kinkaids partook in the questioning, even little Carmella seated beside Lucy. William was on her other side, protectively close.

By now, Lucy had lost track of the assorted construction workers, farmers, and sportsmen with implements in tow, which William had very wisely insisted they leave on the porch. But it was the undertaker who gave her pause, pasty pale in his approach, assuring her that their place was nice and quiet, dark and cool, too. Chill bumps raced down her spine saying, for sure, he wasn't the one. Neither was the pilot asking her to *come fly with me,* the sheik in a turban, or the knight with a proclaimed penchant for the chastity belt!

Finally, here before her sat a reasonable looking person, a mid-thirties naval officer who was really quite handsome, his blue eyes complemented by his uniform.

"I've spent six long months at sea," he said sincerely, "thinking of nothing but you."

Lucy sighed, almost daring to believe it. He seemed decent enough, fine and upstanding. Broadly built across the shoulders, too. She caught William watching her careful perusal of his chest and coughed.

"Where did you say we lived again?" she asked, taking a sip of water Emma had placed on the coffee table for her earlier. All this talking had left her parched. Maybe, here at last, she'd come to her oasis. She looked the officer in the eye and he shared a winning smile.

"In the prettiest little house, with a white picket fence."

"Oh," she said, charmed. "That sounds lovely."

William stroked his chin and glanced at the guy. "White picket fences are a pain, you know," he told Lucy.

Grant leaned forward in his wing chair. "It's true. Have to paint them every year."

"No worries about the little lady lifting a finger," the officer said. "She can leave all the manly work to me."

William shifted uncomfortably as Grant watched his son. Emma surveyed them both before jumping in. "So what about ID?"

The officer turned toward her, confused. "My military credentials? I already showed those."

Grant nodded approvingly at his wife. "Not those. We're talking something more personal."

"Personal?" the man asked.

"You bet," William said.

"Something to prove you're the real McCoy."

"Proof! Yeah, we want proof!" Carmella butted in.

Justin sat nearby watching the show with interest, but didn't say a word. Lucy glanced at him and then at the others.

"Proof's not a bad idea," she said, guessing what the Kinkaids had in mind. She studied her engagement ring a moment and looked the officer in the eye.

"Well now, I was out at sea," he faltered, "I'm not sure how much you think I—"

"You would certainly know your nickname?"

"Nickname?"

"Sure, you know," Lucy said brightly. "Something I might have called you. Something…" She flushed a little inspite of herself. "…intimate between the two of us. A pet name?"

He stared at her, dumbfounded, then searched all of their faces. "Fido?"

William closed the door a few seconds later as Emma spoke. "And to think, it looked like we were getting close there for a minute."

"Harrumph," Grant said, shaking his head. "All a bunch of nut jobs."

"I'm afraid you're right, Dad," William agreed.

Lucy sighed, exhausted. At this rate, they'd never find her true home.

William regarded her sympathetically. "How about we take a break? You look as if you're done for the day, and you still should rest after that whack on the head."

"That would be terrific," she said, feeling her tension ease. Who knew it could be so hard trying to find the man you were in love with? "But what do we tell the others outside?"

"Don't worry," William said, "I'll take care of it."

William stepped out on the porch as Emma and William took Carmella into the kitchen for a snack. Justin lingered behind, eyeing Lucy.

"You've really got them lined up around the block," he said.

"Thanks to your Web page," she said, attempting to be pleasant.

"Naw. I'd said it's thanks to whatever it is Dad's been staring at."

"What do you mean?"

"I think you know what I mean. He's been looking at you all goo-goo-eyed ever since you got here."

"Your dad's just trying to help."

"Yeah, and so are you. Help yourself to this family," he said with a bitter edge.

"Justin, that's not really fair. Nobody wants to know who I am any more than I do, believe me."

"Meanwhile, you've got it awfully cushy not knowing, don't ya? Cushy enough to worm your way into my dad's heart."

Lucy's face warmed. "I... You don't know that's true. Besides, my stay here is only temporary. Very soon I'll have my old life back and be out of your way. But Justin, in the meantime..." She studied him sincerely. "I'd sure like it if you and I could make some sort of peace."

"You mean like, if I'm not nice to you, you'll tell?"

Her shoulders sagged as she hurt for him. She knew the boy was having a rough time, but she honestly wasn't here to make things any tougher. "I'm not saying that it's mandatory."

"Man-da-who?"

"Nothing's mandatory, Justin. I'm not forcing you to do anything, because I know that I can't. You're practically a man now. Old enough to make your own decisions."

He eyed her suspiciously. "Well, if you're not forcing me, just what are you doing?"

"Asking you." She raised her brow. "Pretty please? Your choice."

Just then, William came inside carrying a stack of mail. He looked from Lucy to his son, and then back again. "Is something going on in here?"

Lucy stared at him innocently. "Nothing at all."

William turned toward his son. "Justin?"

"Nothing, Dad. It's nothing, okay?" He turned and ducked into the kitchen, as something in William's stack of mail caught Lucy's eye.

There was a picture of some guy on the back of a real estate brochure. A face with short dark hair and big black eyes floated over a fairy-tale scene, a castle with hot pink turrets. What was it about the banner fluttering from one of the turrets—*Let Magic Maker Mitch Find the Castle of Your Dreams*—that called her up short?

William's voice hummed from far away as her whole world went woozy.

"Bridget? Are you all right?"

She felt a sharp stab of pain above her left temple. "Oh! Oh, my head." Lucy blinked hard, stumbling toward him.

William caught her in his strong arms and shored her up against him. "Bridget? What's wrong?"

Bridget? Why was he calling her that? Lucy felt herself spiraling into a dark tunnel, visions swirling around her: Gus serving up pancakes... Mitch handing her packages... Waking up on the sofa here... And, huh? Her parents dancing to Billie Holiday...?

"I'm... not really me," she breathed as William embraced her.

Sleigh bells sounded as her world went black and something strong lifted her up and carried her away.

William addressed Dr. Mass, his voice tinged with concern. "She's going to be all right, isn't she, Doc?" Beside them, Bridget was stretched out on the sofa, covered by a throw blanket.

"Oh yes, fine," Dr. Mass said. "It's not as bad as it looks. She's just getting over the shock."

"You mean, about who she really is?"

"Could very well be."

"But why would that make her faint?"

Dr. Mass stroked his snowy beard. "At times, these amnesia cases involve some sort of internal conflict. When the memories start to resurface, they're not always a welcome relief."

"You're saying she's scared to face the truth about who she really is?"

"That all depends on what she has to gain—and lose—by becoming herself again."

William cast his gaze on Bridget, slumbering like a beautiful princess. Perhaps he'd been reading too many fairy tales to Carmella, but he couldn't help but think she looked like she'd stepped right out of one of those storybooks' pages. But in the tales he'd read his little girl, it was always a handsome prince that came along. Not some wayward banker with a middle-class mortgage and a couple of kids.

"Dr. Mass," he said, meeting the older man's eyes. "Can I ask you something?"

"Go right ahead."

"Well, I know this sounds crazy. Loony, for sure. Asking you of all people... But something has happened in this house, something that defies all... What I mean to say is—" He drew a breath. "Do you believe in Santa Claus?"

"Believe in Santa Claus? Who me?" Dr. Mass chuckled and thumbed his chest. "Why, of course I do!"

"You what?" William sputtered.

"William, my boy," Dr. Mass said, packing his medical bag, "I've known you your whole life. I've seen you grow from diapers until now, and you've become a very fine man indeed. But somewhere along the line, you changed. I'm not sure when. Maybe it was when you lost Karen. You seemed to lose your faith."

"But, Santa! I'm talking the guy in the red suit!"

"Yes, yes. The one who comes on Christmas Eve. Is that the one you mean?" He snapped his bag shut and looked up. "But see, that's where you've gotten things mixed up."

"Mixed up how?" William asked, perplexed.

"I don't know who on earth started that myth, because that's what it is, a flat-out untruth."

"Aha! So there *is no Santa.*"

Dr. Mass, who'd started toward the door, stopped walking. "There is a Santa Claus, indeed," he said, meeting William's gaze. "But can't you see? He doesn't just exist on Christmas Eve. He's here the whole year through!

"June, September, yes, even in January. It's not so much about the man in the red suit as it is about what's in your heart. All you have to do is open yourself up to the magic and believe."

Emma entered the living room to find William sitting in a wing chair by the sofa.

"Is the doctor gone?"

"Yes."

She quietly shut the kitchen door behind her. "You're really worried about this girl, aren't you, son?"

"I'm worried about her and Carmella, too. About what the truth is going to do to all of us."

"Maybe you shouldn't have lied to Carmella."

"Mother! I never lied!"

"You evaded the truth."

"No, I didn't know it," he said firmly. "In fact, I'm still not sure I do."

She sat in the chair opposite his and spoke with a kind smile.

"Come now, William. You're a little old to believe in Santa."

He longingly studied Bridget, sleeping on the sofa, then met his mother's eyes.

"Am I?"

"What are you saying? That you've fallen in love with a total stranger?"

"I never said that, precisely. Only..."

"What?"

"You know how it's been since Karen died.

Emma studied her son. "Lonely."

"Yes."

"But surely you can't believe—?"

"In miracles, Mother? Why not?"

Just then, Carmella entered and rushed to Bridget's side. "Is she going to be okay, Daddy? Please tell me that she is."

"Yes, sweetie," he assured her, "she's going to be just fine."

The child's face brightened as she turned toward her Grammy. "Did you know she sings really pretty? She sang to me, and it was just like Mommy."

A tear glistened in Emma's eye as she looked from Carmella to her son. "Why not, indeed," she said softly.

Chapter Eight

Mitch hustled toward his desk, where an assistant sat goggling at his computer.

"If you don't mind?" he said, shooing the underling away.

The girl stood and scurried off, casting him an odd look.

Good help really was hard to find. Probably shopping on Q-Bay.

Mitch dropped into his chair with a sigh. Seconds later, his gaze locked on the computer screen. "Sweet Merry Christmas!" he cried aloud. "That's my Luce!" And it was, too, only more bodacious. He'd never known Lucy to go for getups like that. Hey, wait a minute. What did it say? She weren't no mom, for God's sakes. And how could she think her name was Bridget? Was it possible she didn't really know?

Mitch panicked briefly, wondering if this was some sort of trick she was playing. Maybe an attempt to make him reconsider the whole kid thing. Or maybe, just maybe, she was getting back at him. Yeah. That could be it. They were supposed to be together for the holidays, and Mitch suddenly realized he hadn't seen her for five days! *Nope,* he thought shaking his head. *Doesn't seem like my Luce. She don't play no mean tricks. She's a good girl. Really simple.*

He ogled the jingle bell tassels, eyes popping. And now her *simples* was protruding out all over the place. Jesus. Was this any sort of way to behave at the holidays? Mitch quickly crossed himself, hoping his parents hadn't seen. Then he gave the office a slow, studied perusal. Other agents sat at their desks, smirking at their computer screens. They couldn't all be tuned in to this?

"Hey, Magic Maker Mitch!" Amanda called from the front. He'd never liked Amanda. She was always into everybody's business. "You going to go over there?"

Mitch stared at the copy under Lucy's picture seeing an address was listed. Then, ignoring Amanda and the other gawkers, he grabbed his coat and headed for the door.

Grant, Emma, and the kids stood in the foyer, wearing their coats.

"Mom, Dad," William said. "Thanks so much. It's really nice of you to do this."

"Bosh!" Emma said. "The kids love ice-skating. Besides, they need a break from the madness."

"We all do!" Grant proclaimed.

"I don't see why I have to go, too," Justin said with a scowl. "The fuzz brain's the one who likes to skate, not me."

"Just cooperate, Justin," his dad said. "The fresh air will do you good."

"I already got some fresh air."

"You probably shouldn't remind him," Grant whispered gruffly in Justin's ear.

William saw them off from the porch, grateful that the snow had stopped and his lawn had cleared. Even the television trucks had moved on. Thank God. What a circus!

He came back in the house and was surprised to see Bridget sitting unsteadily on the sofa.

"You're up."

She rubbed her eyes and glanced around the room. "Oh, yes. I know this place."

He strode over and sat beside her, gently taking her hand. "Sure, we're in the living room."

"Our living room?" she asked, squinting her eyes.

"No, I'm afraid it's mine."

"No, it's not," She squeezed his hand firmly and met his eyes. "William, it's mine."

He kindly patted the back of her hand with his free one. "I'm afraid you've gotten things confused."

She pulled free of his grip and studied the decor. "Of course, the wallpaper is different."

William ran a hand through his hair. Dr. Mass had been wrong about Bridget. She wasn't getting better. In fact, she seemed even worse! "Bridget, listen to me—"

Blue eyes flashed as she centered her gaze on his. "Why are you calling me Bridget?"

"That's your name, isn't it?"

"No, I don't think so. I mean, it's familiar."

"Do you remember how you got here?"

She gripped the arm of the sofa and stood, staring around her. "That much is a blur. But this place, yes. I remember it. Recall it quite well." Her eyes traveled to the mantel brimming with Christmas decorations, then settled on a spot to the right of the hearth. "Especially the hidden passageway behind the bookcase."

William felt his anxiety spike. She wasn't just confused; now she was growing delusional. "Wait right there. Don't move for a second," he said, snatching his cell off the coffee table. "I think I'd better call Dr. Mass."

"But Chris Mass has already come and gone!"

"You remember that?"

"I thought I heard talking."

William felt himself flush, wondering how much of the conversations she'd overheard. First the one with Dr. Mass and then the one with his mother. "We thought you were sleeping."

She lightly shook her head. "Maybe it was a dream I had. Some talk about Santa Claus?"

William's neck flashed hot. "This will just take a sec," he said, starting to dial. "Why don't you sit until I get back? Just to be sure?"

Lucy took a seat in a wing chair as William slipped from the room. He was trying to whisper, but his voice rose in apparent panic. "What do you mean you can't come? I just told you she's acting delusional! A baby? Well, tell the woman to wait! I don't know. Cross her legs!"

Lucy didn't know much about what was happening, but she didn't believe herself to be delusional. The truth was, everything was getting clearer. So clear, in fact, that now she was certain she'd been right about the bookcase. She stood with determination and steadied herself. While the wood at the back of the built-in shelf had been painted white, she was betting she could still find that loose panel. Lucy carefully moved a few books out of the way, setting them on a lower shelf. *Tap-tap, tap-tap... It was right around... here...* She laid a fingernail under the edge of the panel and tugged lightly. To her amazement, it moved. Gingerly, she slid it sideways. A small dark hollow gaped open. Inside it sat a single switch. She lifted it and loud humming noise sounded. Slowly the bookcase before her began to move.

Lucy stepped back with delight. *I knew it. I just knew it!* Suddenly, everything came back in a flash, as blinding and bright as the whitest snow blizzard. This *was* her house. She had lived here!

William appeared beside her, slack-jawed. "You weren't kidding about that passageway," he said, staring ahead into the cavernous space.

She turned toward him, cheeks aglow. "William," she said. "I know how I got in your house."

He looked at her in disbelief. "Don't tell me you came from in there?"

"I used to play in there all of the time. Just like Nancy Drew."

"Wait a minute. What are you saying? That you used to live in this house?"

"When I was just a kid."

He stared back into the deep, dark tunnel. "Where does this go?"

"Come on," she said, "I'll show you."

She stepped forward and he laid a hand on her shoulder. "Maybe I should go first."

"All right," she said, smiling. Of course this was her house! Something about the shock of hitting her head, and not knowing who she was, must have sent her back to it. Back to the one safe haven she remembered, even if she couldn't recall anything else.

William attempted to scoot past her in the narrow space, bringing them almost chest-to-chest. He paused, looking down into her eyes. "Who designed this place?"

"Someone who used to work for the government. Paranoid schizophrenic, some say."

"Nice."

They were so close, nearly touching, that for a second Lucy couldn't breathe. He was the best-looking man ever, in many respects way more attractive than

Mitch. He had all of the qualities Lucy wanted, everything she'd hoped for in a man. She'd convinced herself he didn't exist. But he did, and here he stood, in the flesh. Funny thing was, they'd never been properly introduced.

"My name's Lucy," she said, her voice coming out as a squeak.

A slow smile worked its way across his handsome face. "That so?"

"Lucy West. I'm a waitress at the diner downtown and live on Ninth Street."

Brown eyes sparkled with delight. "I never thought you were much of a Bridget."

"No."

He studied her for a prolonged beat and for an insane moment Lucy hoped that he might kiss her. She'd harbored the same wish under the mistletoe. Although then, she hadn't fully recalled that she had a fiancé. There was no more denying that now.

"Shouldn't we... You know?" he said, tilting his chin in the direction of the tunnel.

"Yeah, right," she said, stepping back so he could move forward.

At the outdoor skating rink, Justin reluctantly dragged himself onto the ice beside his sister. In a gaggle of girls nearby, one young lady in particular had her eye on the boy. Emma nudged Grant. "Look over there."

"Where?" He craned his neck to spy the pretty brunette giggling into her hand. "Well, I'll be..."

"Do you think Justin has any idea?" Emma asked.

Grant chortled. "Seems like he's going to now."

Emma watched with amusement as the girl skated toward Justin, puffy earmuffs framing the long brown hair flowing behind her as she went. She tapped Justin on the shoulder just as he was about to break into a stride. He turned to stare at the girl in surprise, his neck and the tips of his ears reddening.

"Just like his father," Emma said with a warm smile.

"Hmm," Grant replied. "Looks like she's asking him to skate."

Carmella stood between her brother and the girl, glancing happily from one to the other. "Go on!" Emma heard her shout. "I'm going to have cocoa with Grammy and Poppy."

"I'll come, too," Justin said, racing after her.

The girl's face fell. But then little Carmella took charge. "Oh no you don't," she said, shoving Justin back on the ice. "Not enough cocoa for you."

Justin whirled to face the girl, his whole face beet red.

Grant laughed and then whispered to Emma, as Carmella approached, "Good to see his sister didn't let him chicken out."

Seconds later, the girl held out her hand and Justin took it, letting her drag him onto the ice.

"Looks like Justin's got a girlfriend," Carmella chirped, trudging forward.

Emma and Grant looked at each other and grinned.

Mitch exited his SUV and stormed up the walk to the front door of the Kinkaid house. Something funny was going on here, and whatever it was, he was going to get to the bottom of it. He rang the bell and waited. Then tried again. Nothing doing. Hmm. There was still a car in the drive. Maybe they hadn't heard him, he thought, deciding to use the knocker. Mitch checked his cell for the time, guessing he'd already been standing here ten minutes.

Well, he sure didn't come clear across town for nothing. He laid his hand on the doorknob, turning it easily. Folks should really take more precautions. Leaving your door unlocked these days could only invite trouble.

He tentatively pushed the door open and called inside, but got no response. Maybe they were in the back or were watching television. He walked a few feet indoors and yelled louder. It was then that he saw it, the big gaping hole in the wall. "Sweet Merry Christmas! What's *that?* Looks like somebody bombed this place." Or maybe that's what this was, some sort of bomb shelter. *Yeah, I'm betting that's right. This whole setup just gets weirder and weirder.*

He took a breath and stepped into the darkness.

William laid his hands on the back of the old pegboard, once meant to hold garden tools, and gently pushed. To his amazement, the pegboard popped off in his hands. He grappled to catch it before it spilled forward, then set it aside, leaning it against a nearby wall. "This is incredible," he said, looking around the crowded space. Cobwebs were everywhere inside the old garden shed, several coating the lawn mower.

"Don't do much yard work, do you?" Lucy asked.

He shrugged apologetically. "I hire a lawn service."

"I must have remembered this place," she told him with growing confidence. "Even when nothing else made sense to me. William, this is how I got in your house."

"How long did you live here?" he asked in awe.

"Only until my parents died. I was twelve and a half."

"Oh Lucy," he said, his heart aching for her. "I'm so sorry."

Her eyes misted slightly. "After that, I went to live in a group home. Everyone there was very nice, but it wasn't the same."

Of course, it couldn't have been. How horrible for her to have suffered that tragedy, and at such young age. "Didn't you have any brothers or sisters?" he asked.

"No, it was just me."

No wonder she'd asked about having kids. Perhaps she wanted the sort of family for herself that the fates hadn't allowed her to have as a child. William spoke past the lump in his throat, wishing he could find a way to make things all better. He'd give anything to take away the pain in her eyes at the memory of her loss. "So, it's just you then? You're all alone?"

She drew a breath and forced a brighter look. "No, I've got Mitch."

"Who's Mitch?"

"That would be me," a contentious voice said. "I'm the intended."

William spun in surprise as a stout, dark-haired man stepped out of the passageway and into the crowded space with them.

"Mitch!" Lucy cried with alarm.

"Luce!" he answered, throwing his arms wide. "I thought I'd lost you!" He pulled her into a hug, snug up against him. She shot William a helpless look and his neck flushed hot. What could he do? He couldn't possibly break up the happy reunion.

"Did this fellow hurt you?" Mitch asked, when Lucy pulled back. "Because if he did, I swear—"

"No, Mitch. Seriously. It's not like that at all."

"How is it, then?" he asked, suspiciously eyeing William. In all of his thirty-eight years, William had never felt so entirely sized up.

William stuck out his hand, unsure of what else to do. "I'm William Kinkaid."

Mitch raised an eyebrow at him, then turned back toward Lucy. "Is this on the level? This guy's all right?"

"Yes, Mitch." Lucy sighed heavily. "It's a really long story, but William had nothing to do with me coming here. He's been nothing but the perfect gentleman, I swear."

"Let's hope so," Mitch said, turning to take William's hand. Before he could do it, he stopped. "Wait a minute... What about those, you know..." He cupped his hands in front of his chest. "Jingle bell things."

"That wasn't William," Lucy rushed to explain. "That was Justin."

"Justin? Was this some sort of threesome going on?"

"Mitch!" Lucy shouted in shock.

"Hold on one second," William said, offended. "Justin is my son."

"All the worse!" Mitch's temples bulged and Lucy reached up to sooth them.

"Baby, a lot has happened in this house, but nothing like that. The Kinkaids are a very nice family. They were nothing but good to me."

Mitch scowled, then shook his head. "Well, all right. If you say so." He started to take William's hand again, but stopped. "No monkey business, huh?" he asked Lucy. "Not even with this good-looking ape, here?"

She blushed bright crimson. "No, Mitch."

"Well, good!" He gave her a quick peck on the lips that made William feel slightly sick to his stomach. He'd naturally known all along that Brid—uh, Lucy had a fiancé and another life waiting for her somewhere. He just hadn't realized how unsettling it would be to see it.

Finally, Mitch extended his grip. "Nice to meet you, fellow," Mitch said. "I can't wait to hear this story."

Emma and Grant entered the house holding fast-food bags and sent the kids upstairs to change. As they approached the kitchen, Emma halted, holding up a warning hand to her husband. Grant looked past her to William, sitting glumly at the kitchen table. Emma glanced at Grant with a worried frown. Something didn't feel right in here. Plus, it was awfully quiet.

She put on her sunniest face and carted the burger bags to the kitchen's center island. "We stopped and picked up dinner on the way home."

"Kids already ate in the car," Grant added. "Justin ate like a horse."

William met his parents' eyes with a sad gaze. "Thanks, guys."

"Where's Bridget?" Emma asked.

William sighed and set his palms on the table. "Mom. Dad. I have something to tell you."

Grant walked over and took a seat as Emma slid into another chair.

"What is it, son?" Grant asked.

"Her name's not Bridget," William answered, with red-rimmed eyes. "It's Lucy."

"Well, Lucy's a very nice—" Emma began.

"She's gone."

"Gone?" Grant was visibly surprised.

"Who's gone?" Carmella asked, entering the kitchen.

William stared at his little daughter, hating to break the news. "Bridget, honey. I found out where she lives and—"

"No!" Carmella cried, lunging toward him.

"Hang on, fuzz brain." Justin had appeared and wrapped his arms around her.

She glared at her father, tears streaking down her face. "But it can't be true!"

"Is it, Dad?" Justin asked, his brow creased in concern.

William pursed his lips for a remorseful beat before speaking. "I'm sorry, kids. I wish—"

"But you promised!" Carmella shouted. "*Promised,* Daddy!"

He stood, stepping toward her, but she backed against Justin, who held her tight. Emma's heart broke at the scene. Everyone here was falling apart, not the least of whom appeared to be her son.

"Pumpkin," William said, his voice cracking.

"Don't you 'pumpkin' me!" she said, breaking out of Justin's embrace.

Before they knew it she was through the door, her small footfalls racing upstairs.

"I'll go after her," William told the others.

"Carmella, please honey, talk to me," William said as she hunched forward, burying her face in a pillow. He swallowed past the burn in his throat. "I'm sorry, Carmella. Really, I am."

"But you said she was my mommy!" her muffled voice returned.

William patiently removed the pillow and stroked her damp cheek with his thumb.

"I never said that, sweetheart. You did. I only said I believed in Santa."

"But I don't get it." Pain streaked her eyes, threatening to cleave William in two. "If Bridget's not her real name and Santa didn't bring her... Then..." Her voice faltered again. "There's no Santa at all."

"Now, hang on one second," William said. "We don't know that's so."

"But you can't believe. You just can't. Especially not now."

"Why not?"

"Because he didn't bring you what you wanted, either."

"How do you know what Daddy wanted?"

She stared at him with moistened eyes. "Because I've heard you . . . crying at night." William blinked, turning away. "You wanted somebody, too. Didn't you?"

"Yes," he said in a whisper.

She reached out and touched his arm. "Then, there is no Santa Claus," she said softly. "And if there is, he let us both down."

If that was the truth, then why did Carmella's statement ring so false in his heart? Maybe things hadn't worked out as they might have, but he would never call having had Lucy here a mistake. In fact, having her presence in this house—even if for just a little while—had been the greatest of gifts.

"Oh, I wouldn't say that," William said, pulling his daughter into a hug.

Chapter Nine

Time passed painfully slowly for Lucy. Nothing about it seemed to go right. When she got back to her tiny apartment, it appeared dark and cramped, and absent of holiday cheer. All of the Christmas decorations, including her miniature Christmas tree, were artificial. And each of her potted plants had wilted. She'd never been much of a gardener, anyway. Something like William, she supposed, noting the comparison only further dampened her spirits.

She hadn't realized how attached she'd grown to him until the time had come for her to go. He was just the sort of guy she'd always dreamt of, almost like someone from one of those late-night TV shows. He was an excellent father, too. He was good with his kids, loving yet firm. He was there for them and they knew it, just as his parents remained there for him—and vice versa. Lucy sighed, reliving her moments in that happy home. What the Kinkaids had was a real family, and *family* was a feeling Lucy had nearly forgotten.

She sorted through the mail on the kitchen counter, hoping to find something of interest among the solicitations and bills. She paused, gripping a bright red envelope with no return address in her hands. It could be a Christmas card. Or maybe... just maybe... something from the Kinkaids? Her heart pounded as she recalled the gold flecks in William's eyes. Him holding her under the mistletoe... Their *almost* kiss. She slipped a fingernail under the seal and popped it, then pulled the shiny red foil-covered card from its sleeve. *Hoping Santa's good to you this Christmas* it said on the front.

She flipped it open to read the message inside. *And brings you a bag full of joy.* Then, in his charming scrawl, *Gus.*

Lucy's heart warmed despite her frown. Of course it was from Gus. He always ran a week behind and a dollar short. But he was the best darn boss a girl could hope for. Lucy stared out the window at the drifting snow, realizing how foolish she'd been. Thinking she might actually hear from the Kinkaids in general. William, in particular. Naturally, now that she'd gone, they'd all returned to their lives as normal.

That thought didn't stop her from racing to the door a few hours later when the doorbell rang. She opened it to find a florist standing with a huge white box. "Two dozen of our best," he said merrily. She thanked him with a blush and hurriedly took the box inside, ripping into its card. *This time, I promise, I won't let you down. Love, Mitch.*

Lucy gave a melancholy smile, thinking Mitch wasn't such a bad guy. In fact, he was a great guy, and the right guy for her. While it was true he got distracted at times, he was basically a decent man with a good heart. Someone who cared for her, and probably only overworked himself in order to do right by her. Besides, they'd been going out forever and sort of *fit*. He wasn't a bad man and would treat Lucy right, wouldn't run around on her, or purposely be unkind. Over time, they'd work out the baby thing. Once his business had settled down and he wasn't so stressed, he'd be more willing to talk about it.

Lucy eyes misted at the memory of reading to Carmella by the fire and singing her early morning lullabies. Even Justin had seemed to be coming around. Perhaps slowly, but she had a gut instinct she could break through to him if she just kept trying. But these were silly things to dwell on when she had a wedding to plan. She and Mitch were getting married—*married*—in just a few days. There were so many things to check on, and loose ends to tie up.

Lucy felt a tad guilty for not being overwhelmed with joy at the thought of her upcoming nuptials, but knew that she'd get into it eventually. She was sure that when the big moment came, she could look Mitch in the eye and say *I do* with the hopeful expectation of any bride. The sooner she put the illusion of William meeting her at the top of the aisle instead of Mitch, the better. William was this banker prince, and here she she was, this diner Cinderella. It would do her good to keep her life in perspective and stick with the world she knew. At bottom, it was the only world she had.

William sat by the fire with his parents, sipping eggnog. "I want to thank you both for everything you did to help with Brid—I mean, Lucy."

"Takes some getting used to, doesn't it?" Grant asked.

Emma smiled. "Lucy's a nice name. Comes from Lucille, bearer of light."

"And that's how she was, too," William said thoughtfully. "Just like a candle in a window that had been darkened too long."

"Why son, that's very poetic," Grant said with surprise.

William shot his parents a sad smile. "And the funny thing is, I haven't thought much about poetry, or anything else romantic, in a very long time."

"We know, son," Emma said kindly. "And we've kind of been hoping there'd come a day when those things would change."

"What your mother means is, we've been wondering when the day would come when somebody special would turn your head."

"We just never dreamed she'd get dropped down the chimney!" Emma said.

William set down his drink and stared at her in surprise. "Why Mom, aren't you a little old to believe in Santa Claus?"

"Oh no, honey. It's never too late to…" She swigged from her glass. "…renew one's faith. Is it, Grant?" she asked, glancing at her husband.

Grant drained his glass and winked at William. "Never too late, indeed."

A ways beyond their view and at a high bend in the steps, Justin had been sitting and eavesdropping on their adult conversation. He'd never seen his dad this way, all moping about like he'd lost his best friend. When his mom died, his dad had been tough. Super strong for all of them. Justin saw now that maybe that was because he felt he had to be. On the inside, he must have been hurting. Just as much as Justin and Carmella, in some ways. Maybe more.

Justin pulled the small wallet-size photo of Mary, the pretty girl from the skating rink, from his pocket and studied it. She had the sweetest looking face in all of the seventh grade, and he was betting she'd be the best-looking girl in the eighth, too. If he didn't get her to go with him now, it would be over and done with by high school. All the more athletic and smarter boys would have moved in, leaving Justin out in the cold.

He stared down the flight of steps, imagining his dad's long face. While he couldn't precisely view his profile from his hidden spot on the stairs, he could envision how it might look, his brow all creased with worry, his lips taking a downward turn. Justin returned his gaze to Mary's photo and her beautiful, cheerful smile. When that smile was meant for him it made his guts turn inside out, but in a good way. He guessed when Lucy had smiled at Dad, it had made him feel something similar. Maybe something he hadn't felt in a while. For all of Justin's life, his dad had done stuff for him and the fuzz brain. He was a good dad who loved them a lot. Maybe it was time that they let him know they loved him back.

Justin stealthily rose to his feet and crept back up the stairs, an idea taking hold. He tiptoed to his sister's room and snuck in the door.

"What are you doing?" she asked looking up from her Barbie dolls.

He quietly shut the door and rasped under his breath. "Carmella, I have an idea."

"Oh no you don't," she said, firmly shaking her head. "Your ideas get you in trouble, and I don't want any of that."

"Not even . . ." he asked, with a tempting smile. "If they get Lucy back?"

Forty-five minutes later, Carmella goggled at Justin's computer screen. "Looks really good. Do you think it will work?"

"In getting her attention? You bet." He'd done his best with it, computer program modifications and all. It certainly got the message across.

"I still don't know about that word." She frowned. "*Man-a-tory?* Are you sure she'll know what that means?"

Justin shot her an informed look. "Do reindeers fly?"

Carmella studied her brother. "You're some kind of softie, aren't you?"

"Let's just say I had some growing up to do."

"Does this have something to do with Mary?" she asked astutely.

"I don't know. Maybe."

"Wouldn't hurt to have another girl around. I mean, a grown-up one like Lucy, to ask all those mushy love questions to."

"Love...?" Justin surveyed his sister, wondering how she knew so much. "Go back to bed," he said, playfully swatting the side of her head.

William nearly bumped into Carmella exiting Justin's room. "Well hello, pumpkin." He did a double take. "Wait a minute. Didn't I tuck you in over an hour ago?"

"Uh-huh," she said, staging a yawn. "And I'm really tired."

"Then what...?"

"Oh! I had a little bit of a bad dream, so I went to see Justin."

"And Justin helped you out?" he asked uncertainly. The boy did appear to be turning over a new leaf. "Oh yes!" she said brightly. "All better now!"

"Hmm."

"Well, good night, Daddy," she said, giving him a quick hug around the legs and darting to bed. "Sleep tight!"

"You too, pumpkin," he said, thinking something didn't add up. William rapped lightly at Justin's door, then went in.

Justin sat nonchalantly on the bed, scribbling something on a notepad. William couldn't believe his eyes. Was that Justin—writing poetry?

"Hey Dad. What's up?"

"Uh, I just wanted to... About Carmella...?"

"Oh yeah, the fuzz brain had a bad dream. It's okay, though. I told her the monsters weren't real and that she could leave on the lights."

"Very good of you, Justin, thanks," William said, impressed. Who had taken his snarly preteen and replaced him with somebody older and wiser? Not to mention, a bit kinder to his kid sister?

"Was there something else?" Justin asked, apparently ready to get back to his writing.

William had the sneaking suspicion Justin was up to something. For some odd reason, he suspected it had something to do with girls. "Everything all right?"

"Oh yeah, Dad. Just dandy."

Dandy? "There's nothing you want to tell me about? Nothing you want to discuss?" *Like your raging hormones or possible new interest in girls,* William wanted to ask.

Justin smiled at him, tightlipped. "Nope."

Chapter Ten

William had been pondering a way to see Lucy again, but knew that it wouldn't be right just to pop on over there and say *hi* the day before her wedding. Still, he had her gifts to return. Bridget's gifts, anyway. William peered in the top box, his face firing red. Well, no wonder Lucy hadn't wanted him to look! He paused, wondering what had become of his sense of adventure. He wasn't even forty and yet it seemed he'd morphed into an old man. Something about the light in Lucy's bright blue eyes told him she could find a way to reawaken his youth. Hadn't he nearly been driven to pull her into his arms and carry her up to his bed half a dozen times? Okay, he had carried her upstairs that once. But given that they scarcely knew each other at the time, and she was effectively passed out, that didn't seem to count.

William sat on the side of the bed, feeling foolish. There really hadn't been anyone since Karen died. The fact was, when his wife had gone he'd been so devastated by the entire event, he didn't believe he'd ever love again. And then, this stranger waltzed into his house... More like sleepwalked... And suddenly, his heart was all over itself, unable to stop its pounding each time that she was near. There was something about her, he didn't know what, that just seemed so right. It was like she'd belonged in this house . . . and in his arms, he thought, as his neck flushed hot. Though he never truly got the chance to hold her like he'd yearned to do. He tried to imagine what that might be like, having a wife and mother in this house once more. He'd never before trusted there would be a way for that to work. The person would have to be very special. Extra special. To fit such a large bill.

But what was he doing entertaining such cockamamie notions? Tomorrow, Lucy was marrying Mitch. That was the life she was meant to lead, and had decided on, long before she'd wound up on William's sofa. It wasn't like a few days with his family were going to change her mind.

Lucy trudged through the snow up to William's house, her palms damp inside her warm wool gloves. For the past forty-eight hours, she'd been dreaming up any excuse she could think of to come on over. Then, she recalled Bridget's packages. Of course, she had to get them back and make that delivery. After all, she'd promised Mitch.

Maybe it was true that deep inside she longed to see William again. Ever since staying with the Kinkaids, she'd felt oddly conflicted about her upcoming wedding. Perhaps dropping by this morning would set everything right. She'd had a few days to gather her thoughts and distance herself from the disconcerting events that had occurred here, she thought, climbing the front porch steps. Lucy paused, taking in the pretty handmade Christmas wreath, tied up with a bright red bow and hanging from the front door. Everything in this house teemed with life.

Especially William! She looked up with a start when he opened the door, before she could ring the bell. He stood there in his parka, appearing more handsome than ever, light brown eyes sparkling with surprise. "Lucy!" he said, holding a stack of Christmas gifts.

"Bridget's packages," she exclaimed, heaving a breath. "I was just coming to get them!"

He raised his brow. "You were?"

"Who's at the door, dear?" Emma called from inside. She appeared behind William a few seconds later, followed by Grant.

"Why, Lucy!" she said, rushing over to give her a hug. "What a pleasant surprise."

"Indeed," Grant said with a grin. "In fact, we were just talking about you."

William turned to his parents and parroted with Lucy, "You were?"

"Yes, yes, of course." Emma ushered Lucy inside and shut the door. "Come on in and out of the cold. I just put a pot of coffee on."

Hearing voices downstairs, Justin and Carmella decided to go investigate.

"Carmella, look," Justin whispered at the top of the steps as his Poppy helped Lucy off with her coat and his dad set down a stack of packages.

"Wow," Carmella whispered back. "That worked fast."

Justin nodded. "Guess that's what they mean by *instant upload*."

"Hey kids!" William called upstairs. "Come on down! We've got company!"

Justin and Carmella smiled at each other, beginning their rapid descent.

"Justin! It's so good to see you," Lucy said with a happy grin. "And you know, I have something to tell you. I'm not mad at all about that Web page."

Justin glanced at Carmella, then spoke, his voice lightly cracking. "That's great!"

"I know you kids were only trying to help," Lucy said sweetly.

Carmella beamed from ear to ear.

Lucy bent low and held out her arms to the little girl. "Come here, you."

Carmella rushed over and gave her a happy hug, as Justin's heart brimmed. He studied his father, who appeared equally pleased that Lucy was here. Sometimes it was nice to do a good thing.

"Let's all head into the kitchen, why don't we?" Emma said. "Gingerbread's in the making."

"Oh boy!" Carmella crowed.

Justin approached Lucy as she neared the threshold and spoke in a low, confident manner. "Good to see you, Luce."

She stared at him, her cheeks aglow. "Why Justin, that's very nice of you to say. It's awfully good to see you, too."

William sat in the kitchen with the others, thinking how good it was having Lucy back in this house. As they sat around the kitchen table, laughing companionably and sharing warm gingerbread, it was almost as if she belonged here.

"I thought the farmer was a hoot," Grant said, as they relived happy memories.

"I liked the knight on the horse," Emma said.

Justin sipped from his cocoa. "I liked the paratrooper."

"Yeah, well, I liked Daddy best!" Carmella chirped, looking around.

The adults chuckled as Lucy hung her head with a blush.

She looked up, meeting William's eyes, and his heart skipped a beat. "You really were the best out of all of them... I mean, as far as keeping everything organized. I don't know how I could have managed without you."

"William's very good at organizing things," Emma said.

"And he's an excellent provider," Grant piped in.

The tips of William's ears burned hot as Lucy's cheeks colored. "Yes, well..." William stumbled with the words. "The important thing is that we provided a place for Lucy when she was lost."

"Confused was more like it," she said. "I'm so very grateful to all of you. For taking me in and making me feel so much at home."

"It's amazing that this was your house once," Emma said.

"Yes," Lucy agreed. "It seems I have a happy history here."

"History has a way of repeating itself," Grant said with a knowing look.

What were his parents driving at? It was almost embarrassing the way they were throwing themselves at Lucy, dropping hints here and there concerning everyone's feelings for her. Including his own, he acknowledged, sentiment overtaking him. Here she was, this wonderful, beautiful woman, whom his parents and his kids obviously adored. And she was getting hitched to another man.

"You know, we've been thinking," Emma said as she stood to refill the adults' coffees, "Grant and I..." She cast her husband a look. "That, with the New Year upon us, it would be terribly good to get together and celebrate."

"At our house for a change," Grant added. "You know, card games, puzzles. Champagne at midnight. A good old-fashioned family New Year's Eve."

"Yes, dear," Emma said, her expectant gaze on Lucy's. "And we were hoping you could join us."

Lucy's eyes brimmed with gratitude. "That sounds lovely," she said. "Really special. You don't know how much I'd like to come. But I can't." She set down her mug resolutely, then looked around the room, taking them in one by one. "I'm afraid that I'm getting married tomorrow night at eight o'clock."

"Married?" everyone but William cried.

"Didn't William tell you?"

Grant studied his son. "No, I'm afraid he left that little detail out."

"Where is the ceremony, dear?" Emma asked kindly.

"Up at the Old North Church, out on River Road."

"Of course, we know it," Emma said. "Sweet little place."

"If I could, I'd invite you all," Lucy said. "But the chapel's small, and it's only family."

"Naturally, we understand." Emma took her seat with a heavy heart. William felt as if someone had ripped his heart from his chest and replaced it with a huge iron anchor.

William turned toward Lucy, sinking into the depths of her eyes. They were beautiful eyes, angel eyes. *But this Christmas angel belongs to someone else,* William reminded himself. "And we wish you and Mitch the very best," he said quietly.

Justin rubbed his forehead as Carmella watched her father with a frown.

Grant stood and warmly patted Lucy's shoulder. "Of course, we do. Congratulations. From all of us."

Chapter Eleven

Lucy stood glumly before her mirror applying the last of her makeup. Well, this was it. The big day had arrived. She studied her reflection, deciding she looked passable in the simple wedding dress she'd bought online. Mitch would never guess it was a second. The important thing was, she was wearing it for the first time with him. Lucy sighed and pulled on her heavy coat, expecting him at any minute.

She noted the light was blinking on her answering machine and hit *play*.

"Hey sugar, it's me, Gus," his voice said. "Don't get me wrong here. I'm still pleased as punch to be walking you down the aisle tonight, but all of us over at the diner found something on the Internet we think you should take a look at."

Moments later, Lucy sat at her PC typing in the URL Gus had provided. The page loaded and her eyes watered, threatening to overflow. Clearly this was something Justin had crafted, probably with Carmella's help.

There was a Kinkaid family picture and her figure had been cut and pasted in. The caption read: *Sexy Cyber Dad Seeks Mom. Only those answering to "Lucy" and perfectly matching this photo's description need apply. Personal experience with Santa and his reindeer team a plus. Extra room in her heart for two great kids mandatory.*

"Crazy, adorable kids," she said, as tears escaped her.

Mitch knocked at the door and she nabbed some tissues off a nearby table to dab her weepy eyes. She had to pull herself together. The man who loved and wanted her was just outside and prepared to whisk her away and into a new and happy life. She would be happy, wouldn't she?

"Wow, you look gorgeous," Mitch said as she opened the door.

"You don't look so bad yourself," Lucy answered. And he didn't. Mitch had cleaned up very well, and looked really nice in his tuxedo and red rose boutonniere.

"So, ready to go and do this thing?" he asked with a grin.

Lucy forced a shaky smile. "You bet."

"Great. That makes two of us." He held out his arm to escort her. "Your carriage awaits!"

"Mitch?" she began tentatively.

"Yeah?"

"Have you ever tried blueberry pancakes with chocolate syrup on top?"

"Ew! That's disgusting! Why would you ask...? Wait a minute. You're not trying to prep me up for some of those pregnancy cravings, are ya?"

Lucy cast a sorrowful gaze toward her computer. "I can't really have the kids without the father, can I?"

"Now, you're talking crazy, Luce." He stopped walking and turned toward her. "Are you all right?"

"Yes, fine." She pulled herself upright and looked him in the eye. "I'm sorry, Mitch. I just had a weak moment, but it's passed. I know what I want to do."

The mood was grim at the senior Kinkaid house. Grant and Emma couldn't get anybody to do anything.

Justin didn't want to play cards and Carmella refused to work puzzles. Finally, the grandparents gave up and turned on the television, letting the kids watch a New Year's Eve show, complete with stage performers and marching bands.

William was sure his mom had cooked a delicious dinner, but the truth was that he hadn't been able to taste a bite. It was like his whole world was in a haze and he was detached from everything. He'd meant what he'd said to Dr. Mass when he questioned the older man about Santa Claus. Something unusual, magical, had happened when Lucy arrived. And when she'd gone, she'd taken all that brightness with her, leaving him in this dark well of despair. How could it be that the fates had brought home just the right person for him... for all of them.. and then just as suddenly snatched her away?

William looked up from where he sat on the sofa and Grant motioned him into the kitchen—and out of the earshot of the others.

"Want a drink, son?" his dad asked gruffly.

William glanced at the still untouched glass in his hand. "Thanks, I've got one."

Grant met his gaze. "How about something stronger? A kick in the ass?"

"Dad!" William said with surprise.

Grant massaged his chin and studied William. "You know, son, we Kinkaids might be many things, but I've never thought of any of us as quitters."

"Quitters?"

"Just look at yourself. All moping about and giving up, while the woman of your dreams goes waltzing down the aisle with someone else."

"That's just it! She's already marrying someone else."

His dad shot him a disappointed look. "Well, fine. Okay, then. Just throw in the towel if that's how you feel. If you really, in your heart, believe Lucy's making the right decision.

"But if you believe, even for a second, that she's making the wrong one, don't you think you owe it to yourself—and her—to go out there and tell her so?"

Gus and Lucy stood at the top of the short aisle. The small chapel was lovely, still decorated for Christmas with candles and holiday greenery. Mitch waited up front, beaming brightly beside the waiting priest.

"Remember," Gus said, taking her arm. "Just keep it nice and steady."

"Thanks for being here, Gus."

He leaned toward her, speaking under his breath. "I feel like I'm walking you to your execution."

"Sometimes you have to take what life serves you up," she whispered back, "even if it gives you indigestion."

"Right, but I won't tell Mitch that you said that."

William stared at his father, affronted. "Dad, are you calling me a wimp?"

"Why, yes. Yes, I suppose I am."

William set his jaw, knowing one thing firmly. He wasn't some coward who backed down from a challenge. Never had been. Who was he to step aside and assume Mitch was the right guy for Lucy? Shouldn't he let her decide that for herself?

"Now, I know things have been tough since—" his dad went on.

"Hold that thought," William said, nabbing his keys off the counter. Damn straight Lucy should decide things for herself. But how on earth could she, when she hadn't even been presented with a choice?

"Atta boy!" Grant called, as William raced from the room. "Go get her!"

Emma and the kids stared at him, stunned, as he yanked on his parka and bolted for the door. "Be back soon," he said, as their faces all brightened in smiles.

William rushed through the snow to his SUV, noting it was coming down heavily again. He held up an arm to shield his eyes from the onslaught. When he was nearly to his driveway, a cascade of heavy wet flakes poured down on him "What on earth?" He squinted heavenward, almost swearing he'd heard sleigh bells. "No," he said, shaking his head. "No earthly way."

Ten minutes later, William burst through the door of the chapel covered in white flakes. "Hang on just one second!" he shouted. "I object!"

The priest eyed him curiously as he bustled his way to the front. "I'm afraid, young man, we haven't yet gotten to that part."

Lucy blushed mightily. "William!" she cried with unmasked delight.

"You!" Mitch declared, not nearly as happy to see him.

A man stood from the front pew. From his looks, he appeared to be Mitch's father. "What's the meaning of this?" he demanded.

"The meaning of this, sir," William said as he pressed his way to the front, "is that something's happening here that maybe shouldn't be."

Mitch's mother addressed him. "What's he talking about, son? Do you know this man?"

"I do!" Lucy shouted, nearly breathless. Boy, she was gorgeous in the pretty white dress. Just like a picture straight from heaven.

Mitch to turned her. "Hey! I thought there was no monkey business going on!"

"There wasn't," William stated calmly. "But that didn't prevent me from developing feelings for Lucy. Very deep feelings."

"You did? I mean, you have?" Lucy asked with a hopeful blush.

"I do," William said, his voice growing froggy.

"Oh my," the priest said.

"Hoo boy," Gus echoed.

Mitch spoke to Lucy, hurt etched in his voice. "Wait a minute. You can't possibly be saying that you love this guy?"

"Oh Mitch, I'm so terribly sorry. I never meant for it to happen."

"Was that a yes?" the priest asked.

"Was it, Lucy?" William asked, his eyes on hers.

"But Luce," Mitch inserted. "We... you said..."

She studied him kindly. "We said so many things. But can't you see? Neither of us really knew what we were talking about. You said you never wanted kids, and I agreed. Not because that's how I really felt but—"

Mitch blinked hard. "Are you saying you would have tricked me?"

"Tricked you? Never. But would I have tried to convince you to change your mind? Over time? Then yes, I'm sure. And when I realized I couldn't because that's how you really feel, then I would have made the two of us miserable."

"But you said I was the only baby you need."

"I know what I said, but I was wrong." She glanced lovingly at William. "Wrong about so many things. I didn't really know what having children was like until I had a chance to live that life for myself. It helped me understand how important that is to me."

"And she's going to make a wonderful mother, too," William interjected.

Mitch's cell buzzed and he reached a hand in his pocket to answer it. "Sorry folks," he said, checking the number. "Business." He pressed talk. "Magic Maker Mitch, at your service!"

Mitch's parents turned to each other and sighed while the priest drew a breath.

William smiled at Lucy and she grinned broadly in return.

"There's still a party invitation with your name on it," he said.

Lucy shot the small crowd an apologetic look, then took William's hand, as they raced down the aisle and into the dressing room to grab her things.

William and Lucy dashed out of the church and into the snow, where he pulled her into his arms. "I couldn't let you go through with it," he said as snow fell around them. "Not knowing what I know now, and how strongly I feel. The moment you walked into my world, Lucy, everything changed. And if that's not magic, then I don't know what is." He dove into her eyes, wanting to stay there forever. "Up until this year,

I'd long ago given up believing in Santa Claus. I know it sounds crazy, but now I—"

She reached up and lightly stroked his cheek. "I know. I believe, too."

He settled his arms around her, holding her close. "I love everything about you, Lucy West. The way you eat your blueberry pancakes and burn the bacon... The way you are with Carmella and somehow broke through to Justin... The way you charmed my parents, and also me."

Tears glistened in her eyes. "And I've fallen for you, William. All of you. I never really knew what having a family of my own was like until I found you. And now that I do, I can't imagine a life without it."

"Then *don't*. Marry me, Lucy. Be my bride."

"Oh William," she said with a happy gasp, "if I had a whole yard full of grooms to choose from, I'd pick you."

"I'm glad," he said, closing the distance between them with a kiss. Her lips met his, warmly and willingly. He deepened his ardor and she returned it, every bit the taste of heaven he'd imagined.

Somewhere high above them, music chimed.

"Did you hear that?" she asked, pulling back. "It almost sounded like... bells?"

"Did it now?" he asked with a happy laugh. She was incredibly beautiful, so warm and feminine against him, and she was going to be his. *His bride* forever. Yearnings stirred within him he hadn't felt in a while. And boy, was he eager to make good on them. He bent low to scoop her into his arms, billowy white gown, winter coat, and all.

"I'm awfully glad you landed on my sofa," he said with a husky rasp. "You're welcome back there any time."

She wrapped her arms around his neck and hugged him tightly as he carried her toward his SUV. "If that's an invitation, I accept."

"Shall we head back and tell my folks and the kids?"

She shot him a mysterious smile that made his heart soar. "Something tells me they already know."

Not far away, Grammy and Poppy stood with the kids, peering out their bay window.

"That's funny," Emma said. "I could have sworn I heard something. How about you, Grant?"

He shook his head and stared outdoors. "Just a slight ringing in my ears."

"Well, I heard it," Carmella said. "And I know who it was, too."

"Don't be silly, fuzz brain," Justin said, but this time with affection. Just then, he saw a flash of light up in the sky and something far away, trailing off into the night. "Oh no, no... no."

"What is it, Justin?" Grammy asked.

"Just been gaming too much, that's all."

"Sure," Carmella said. "But you know that there's a Santa because you got what you wanted, too."

"Yeah? What's that?"

"The same thing that I did," she said confidently.

"How do you know so much?" Justin asked.

"I asked Grammy and Poppy about *man-a-tory*."

Justin pursed his lips to steel his emotions. The truth was, he hadn't thought he was ready for a new mom, and didn't even believe he wanted one. When

Lucy came along, though, everything had changed. "Do you think she said yes?" he asked his grandparents.

Emma and Grant exchanged glances and grinned. "Do reindeers fly?" they said together.

THE END

A Note from the Author

Thanks for reading *The Holiday Bride*. I hope you enjoyed it. If you did, please help other people find this book.

1. This book is lendable, so loan it to a friend who you think might like it so that she (or he) can discover me, too.

2. Help other people find this book: write a review.

3. Sign up for my newsletter so that that you can learn about the next book as soon as it's available. Write to GinnyBairdRomance@gmail.com with "newsletter" in the subject heading.

4. Come like my Facebook page: http://www.facebook.com/GinnyBairdRomance.

5. Comment on my blog: The Story Behind the Story at http://www.goodreads.com.

6. Visit my website: http://www.ginnybairdromance.com for details on other books available at multiple outlets now.

www.ingramcontent.com/pod-product-compliance
Lightning Source LLC
Chambersburg PA
CBHW052300220925
33019CB00027B/203